D1526243

RAISING THE ANTE

THE KINGS: WILD CARDS BOOK 2

CHARLIE COCHET

Raising the Ante

Copyright © 2020 Charlie Cochet

http://charliecochet.com

All rights reserved. No part of this book may be reproduced or transmitted in any form or by any means, electronic or mechanical, including photocopying, recording, or by any information storage and retrieval system without the written permission of the author, except for the use of brief quotations in a book review.

This is a work of fiction. Names, characters, places, and incidents either are the products of author imagination or used fictitiously. Any resemblance to actual persons, living or dead, business establishments, events, or locales is entirely coincidental.

Cover content is for illustrative purposes only. Any person depicted on the cover is a model.

Cover Art Copyright © 2021 Reese Dante

https://reesedante.com/

Edits by Desi Chapman, Blue Ink Editing

https://blueinkediting.com

Proofing by Brian Holliday, Blue Ink Editing

https://blueinkediting.com

** Please note this story contains scenes dealing with sensitive issues that may trigger some readers. While not graphic, scenes include characters discussing sexual assault and suicide.

FOUR KINGS SECURITY UNIVERSE

WELCOME to the Four Kings Security Universe! The current reading order for the universe is as follows:

FOUR KINGS SECURITY UNIVERSE

STANDALONES
Beware of Geeks Bearing Gifts - Standalone (Spencer and Quinn. Quinn is Ace and Lucky's cousin) Can be read any time before *In the Cards*.

FOUR KINGS SECURITY
Love in Spades - Book 1 (Ace and Colton)
Ante Up - Book 1.5 (Seth and Kit)
Free short story

Be Still My Heart - Book 2 (Red and Laz)
Join the Club - Book 3 (Lucky and Mason)
Diamond in the Rough - Book 4 (King and Leo)
In the Cards - Book 4.5 (Spencer and Quinn's wedding)
Free short story

FOUR KINGS SECURITY BOXED SET

Boxed Set includes all 4 main Four Kings Security novels: Love in Spades, Be Still My Heart, Join the Club, and Diamond in the Rough.

THE KINGS: WILD CARDS

Stacking the Deck - Book 1 (Jack and Fitz)
Raising the Ante - Book 2 (Frank and Joshua)
Sleight of Hand - Book 3 (Joker and Gio)

RUNAWAY GROOMS SERIES

Aisle Be There - Book 1 (King's cousin Gage)

SYNOPSIS

Former firefighter Frank Ramirez has never been afraid of the heat until it came in the form of the sweet and sinful Joshua Sterling.

Frank's days of rushing into burning buildings might be behind him, but as the owner of one of the most prestigious gay nightclubs in Florida, he's still putting out fires. Lately, it's been one disaster after another, making Frank grumpier than usual. If that wasn't enough, someone is out to sabotage his business.

Joshua has a plan. He's done pining after the man of his dreams and ready to do something about the sizzling attraction between them. He sets out to help Frank, and as executive assistant to billionaire Colton Connolly—and friend to his mayhem-magnet husband—Joshua knows a thing or two about managing chaos.

When a hidden threat raises the stakes, Joshua and Frank are put to the test. Can they win the fight for their love... and their lives?

ONE

THIS WAS A NIGHTMARE.

Frank rubbed his temples, hoping to ease the growing ache. He sat back in his chair with a heavy sigh, his eyes narrowing at the blue feather that delicately floated to the carpet of his usually pristine office to join the other dozen or so that had accumulated in the last ten minutes. Damn feather boas shed just from looking at them.

Much like his office, the sleek black surface of his desk resembled a small warzone where chaos had been the clear victor. A twitch in his right eye had him pressing a finger to it. His office had become a ramshackle staging area for his club's upcoming Winterland Gala—one of the club's biggest events of the year, next to its charity masquerade.

Sapphire Sands threw several lavish parties throughout the year, many benefitting LGBTQA+ charities. No event, no matter how perfectly planned, went off without a hiccup or two, but this one decided to declare diva status and become the biggest pain in his ass, starting with this morning's burst pipe in the employee lounge.

With current repairs making the lounge unusable for who the hell knew how long, they'd relocated the staff to the next adequately sized room, meaning the props, decorations, and costumes were moved out of the club's staging area and crammed into storage closets. The leftover decorations, along with racks of costumes, were moved into Frank's office. He would have welcomed the intrusion of feathers and sequins were it the only problem he faced.

"This is what I get for giving Alejandro time off. Why didn't you talk me out of it? Can't we call him back in?"

From his spot on the black leather sofa on the other side of Frank's desk, Seth pressed his lips together like he was trying hard not to laugh. The bastard.

"Sure, Frank. I mean, he's kind of in the middle of his honeymoon, but let's call and say we need him to leave his new husband in Paris so he can come home to put out your fires. Wait, weren't you a firefighter in another life? Isn't putting out fires what you do?"

Frank leveled his unimpressed gaze on Seth. "You know, you've gotten awful mouthy since you got promoted to house manager."

Seth let out a bark of laughter. "You mean since we became friends and I realized you weren't actually a fire-breathing dragon?"

"Dragons are very sexy," Kit pitched in from the floor, where he sat adding translucent glitter to a giant Styrofoam snowflake, his platinum blond hair sporting several stray glitter specks.

Frank was very confused. "Your boyfriend isn't making any sense."

"Don't mind him," Seth replied, shaking his head in obvious amusement. "He's obsessed with gay dragons right now."

"I don't want to know," Frank muttered. "What I *do* want to know is where the hell the new event manager is. The event company was supposed to send a replacement *before* Alejandro left." He waved two handfuls of documents at Seth. "Look at all this shit. We have *the* biggest winter event of the year happening in four weeks, and not only does our old event company disappear into the fucking night, but the new company—who's assured us everything would be taken care of, by the way—hasn't even sent me a fucking event manager!"

Technically they *had* sent an event manager. The guy had been a disaster. Didn't know what the fuck he was doing, and Frank told him as much. They were supposed to send someone competent the next day. A week later and Frank was still waiting.

"It's okay," Seth said, his tone soothing as he held up his hands. "It's going to be just fine. We'll work through this."

Thank God for Seth. He was a force to be reckoned with, despite his friendly smile and laid-back nature. He'd quickly become Frank's right-hand man, someone Frank could depend on to help maintain their reputation as the most exclusive members-only gay nightclub in the state.

Frank took a deep breath through his nose and let it out slowly through his mouth. Seth was right. This was a minor inconvenience. So what if he didn't have decorations, tables, chairs, settings, a catering company, menu, price list, flower arrangements, or *anything* he needed for one of his club's most anticipated events? Sure, the invitations had been sent out months ago, and all his clients who'd be in attendance already RSVP'd. No big deal. For years he'd risked his life running into burning structures. He could handle an event gone wrong.

It wasn't as if things hadn't gone wrong in the past. He'd been doing this for fourteen years. Jesus Christ, he was getting too old for this shit. His cellphone rang and he picked up. "What is it, Davie?"

"There's been a delivery, and, um... I think you need to come out here."

"What now?" Perfect. One more thing to add to his list. Fine. It was fine.

"You really need to see it," Davie murmured. Something about his tone sent a deep sense of foreboding through Frank.

"On my way." With a sigh, Frank hung up and stood. "There's a problem out on the floor." He left the office with Seth and Kit on his heels. In addition to Seth, he reminded himself he had Kit, the club's dance choreographer. Of course Kit needed the extra dancers he'd hired for the event to show dance moves to, and the event company had yet to send those either.

Whatever awaited Frank, he'd deal with it as soon as possible so he could move on to the next disaster. Leaving the back of house area, he headed for the club's dance floor.

His blood pressure spiked—he could feel it—when he saw the monstrosity taking up half the dance floor. "The fuck is that?" Frank stopped and stared.

"It's a snowman."

Frank held a warning finger up to Davie, his eyes still glued to the eighteen-foot snowman that he sure as shit hadn't ordered.

"Why does it look surprised?" Kit asked, coming to stand to Frank's right.

"More importantly, why is it holding its crotch?" Seth asked from his left. He pointed to the blue mittens pressed against the snowman's front. That, coupled with the snowman's O-shaped mouth, concerned Frank. Greatly.

"Do snowmen have crotches?" Davie asked as he moved around the snowman. "There's a button back here."

Frank threw out a hand. "Don't you touch a damn—"

The most horrific guttural moan pierced the air seconds before a torrent of white glitter exploded from the snowman's crotch, slamming into Frank with such force it threw him off his feet. He soared through the air and hit the floor hard, his world reduced to a haze of sparkling white.

"Holy shit!" Seth appeared, hovering over him, his dark curls dusted with white glitter and his brows knit together in concern. "Are you okay?"

Frank didn't move. He simply lay there, staring at the ceiling as snowman jizz continued to float down around him. "Seth, be honest with me."

"Of course."

"Did a snowman just ejaculate on me? Is that what happened?"

Seth's lips quivered. He shook his head, lips pressed together as his face turned red from his obvious attempt to hold back his laughter. Other than the noises coming from Seth as he valiantly tried not to burst, the place had plunged into silence. Everyone had cleared out—most likely scrambling to the nearest safe place to lose their shit and laugh their asses off.

Taking Seth's outstretched hand, Frank got up with a groan, his body aching. Layers of white glitter drifted to the floor, and he glared down at his once pitch-black Armani suit.

"I fucking hate glitter," Frank growled as he attempted to brush the glitter off his suit. All that did was add an extra layer of white to his palms. "¡Me cago en diez, hijo de puta!"

Seth's eyes went huge. "Shit. We've reached the Spanish cursing stage. Kit—"

"I'll grab the Beluga Gold." Kit hurried off to grab Frank's favorite bottle of vodka. It was going to be one of those nights.

First things first. "Get that... *thing* out of here. The glitter too. I'm going to change." The club opened in a little over an hour.

"On it."

Seth darted off, and Frank shook as much glitter off as he could before heading into the back of house. He opened the double doors and froze. *Fuck. My. Life.* He'd completely forgotten about his pre-opening meeting with the staff, which he shouldn't have, seeing as how he'd been conducting these meetings every night since he'd opened the damn club.

Two rows of wide eyes stared at him, though no one dared so much as blink, much less crack a smile. Stepping through the doors, he laced his fingers in front of him and addressed his staff like he always did, ignoring the waves of glitter that flowed from his person every time he moved his arms. A speck of glitter fell onto his eyelash, the light hitting it just right and almost blinding him.

"Motherf—" He quickly composed himself. Maybe if he squinted a few times, the little fucker would fall off. Nope. It hung in there.

"Let me, um..." Ruby, one of his go-go boys, slowly inched closer. "I'll just, uh, get that for you." He reached up and carefully plucked the blinding speck off Frank's eyelash.

"Thanks. As I was saying, I should hear back from the event company soon. Once I have the details ironed out, I'll get the schedule up. Have a good night and stay safe."

They all murmured their thanks before hurrying off like someone had lit their asses on fire. He considered undressing in the hall, but his office had already been invaded by all manner of sparkly, fluffy things. Inside, he closed the door behind him and got undressed, remaining in his black boxer-briefs in the hopes of keeping the spread of glitter as far from his private bathroom as possible.

Grabbing a roll of paper towels and a bottle of baby oil from the closet, he started the painstaking process of removing the glitter from his person. By the time he was done and dressed in one of the three black suits and shirts he kept in his office wardrobe,

Kit had knocked on his door. He smiled brightly as he held up Frank's favorite vodka.

IT TOOK the staff almost an hour to get rid of the glitter on the dance floor—though they all knew it would never truly be gone—and deflate the obscene snowman with permanent orgasm face.

"I see what happened," Seth said an hour later from the sofa, tablet in hand. "When Alejandro entered the SKU number for the Giant Snow Confetti-Filled Bauble reversed the last two numbers, which is how we ended up with, um... Frosty Surprise."

"We were definitely surprised," Kit said with a snort. "In more ways than one."

Frank took a seat behind his desk. "I'm glad to hear my unfortunate experience brings you amusement."

"And will continue to do so for years to come. Pun intended." Kit waggled his dark eyebrows, and Frank groaned. He looked to Seth, who blinked at his boyfriend before letting out a loud laugh.

When had he started to lose his touch? At one time Kit and Seth had jumped at his approaching footsteps. Now they made themselves comfortable in his office and tortured him with terrible puns.

"There must have been a malfunction," Seth said, studying his tablet. "Frosty Surprise was supposed to release a soft puff of..." He snorted. "Snowman essence."

"It does not say that." Kit jumped to his feet from where he'd been sitting on the floor working on another giant snowflake. He darted over to his boyfriend and dropped onto the couch beside him. "Oh my God, it does say that!" He keeled over onto his side in a fit of laughter. "Snowman essence!"

"Anyway, it's supposed to release a soft puff, not a jet stream capable of taking out a two-hundred-pound man."

"I had an ex-boyfriend with that problem," Kit mused. "My boss sent me home from work the next day because he thought I had pink eye."

"Wait a minute." Frank remembered that day. "That was me."

Seth eyed Frank. "You shot in his eye?"

"What? No!" Frank glared at Kit, who absolutely no help at all. Why he found this whole thing hilarious was anyone's guess. "I'm the one who sent him home."

Before Kit had been hired as the club's dance

instructor and choreographer, he'd been one of Frank's go-go boys. The club dancers were off-limits to everyone, both client and staff, but there'd been no way to stop Kit from falling for Seth. Quite literally. The guy fell off his plinth during a routine because he'd been distracted by the handsome bartender. Thankfully Seth had seen Kit dancing too close to the edge and broke Kit's fall.

Despite them insisting nothing was going on, Frank knew better. The two were ridiculous in their attempts to avoid each other, and soon it became obvious Frank had to intervene. So he'd fired Kit.

Frank never did anything without a good deal of thought. Kit was an exceptionally talented dancer, working his way to opening his own dance studio. Suddenly, a better opportunity presented itself. Frank rehired Kit as the club's dance instructor and choreographer. With all the events and parties the club hosted, it made more financial sense for him to just hire his own. Seth often teased Frank, insisting he was a romantic at heart, and Frank would promptly tell him to fuck off.

"Right. Time for me to make the rounds," Seth said. He popped a kiss on his boyfriend's mouth before standing. "Frosty Surprise is packed up and in the loading bay awaiting pickup tomorrow morning."

"Perfect." Frank stood and buttoned his suit jacket, frowning when Seth stopped beside him, his lips twitching at the corners. "What?"

"You, um, have a little something on your nose."

Frank ran a finger over his nose. "I fucking *hate* glitter."

With a chuckle, Seth left the office, and Frank followed, leaving Kit to his decorating. The club had just opened for the night, and although not packed yet, it was still busy, with plenty of clients enjoying after-dinner drinks, many still in their business suits. Frank greeted each one personally, shook their hands, told them to have a good night. The go-go boys would be out in the next hour to join guests and keep them company before they hit the plinths for their routines.

By ten o'clock, the club was packed. Frank helped out behind the bar and delivered drinks to his clients. Thursday nights were the start of the weekend, so things would just get busier from here on out. He'd never been one of those absentee club owners who left everything to his manager or staff. Not because he didn't trust Seth to run things for him, but because Frank had built this club from the ground up. His steady presence, imposing to some, also offered a sense of security.

"Frank! *Frank!*"

What the hell? Frank turned, his frown deepening at the panicked look on Seth's face as he hurried through the crowd toward him. Seth didn't panic. The man was a study in control. And why wasn't he using the com? Frank calmly left the bar and stood to one side, away from anyone who might overhear. When Seth reached him, he said the two words no club owner ever wanted to hear.

"Police raid!"

Fuck! Frank rushed toward the front doors just as they slammed open and a small hoard of uniformed police officers flooded in. His stride didn't falter as he growled at Seth. "Call Mason, and get Cory down here."

Seth ran off to call the former officer turned detective who now worked for Four Kings Security, and Cory, Frank's lawyer. Frank did his best to reassure his clients as he headed for the detective in charge, one he didn't recognize. Frank prided himself on maintaining good relationships, especially with local law enforcement. Many of them knew him from his days with the fire department. If they didn't personally know him, they knew of him.

"What's going on?"

"Frank Ramirez?" The sneer on the guy's face

told Frank all he needed to know. Whoever the hell this hotshot was, he'd already formed opinions of Frank and his business, not that Frank gave a shit. What he did give a shit about was the police raiding his club and upsetting his clients.

"Yes. What's this about?"

"We're shutting you down."

TWO

ABSOLUTE PERFECTION. It was a thing of beauty, really.

"I've outdone myself," Joshua said to no one in particular. Or at least he thought no one until someone loomed over him.

"Wow. That's... that's impressive."

Joshua preened under his boss's praise. "Thanks." He took joy in knowing he did a good job, and no one appreciated his skills more than Colton Connolly, president and CEO of Connolly Maritime Enterprises and Worldwide Shipping Solutions. Joshua had been an executive assistant for Connolly Maritime for over two years, but it was only a little over four months ago that he'd been promoted to

Colton's executive assistant, right in time to help the man with his insane wedding schedule.

There'd been a few close calls and several sleepless nights, many of which included coordinating events with Four Kings Security, where Colton's husband, Ace, was part owner. But they'd made it through, and it had been everything the couple hoped it would be, sans complications.

Being the right-hand man to a billionaire was challenge enough. Being the right-hand man to Colton and his makeshift family of former Green Berets and their boyfriends was a whole other level of challenge. At times Joshua wanted to strangle them, but he wouldn't change a thing. Colton wasn't just his boss, he was a friend, and because of that friendship, Joshua had been brought into the Four Kings family.

"I didn't think it was possible," Colton said, sounding a little awed, "but it's even bigger than mine."

"Words I never expected to hear come out of my husband's mouth while bent over another guy."

Joshua lifted his gaze to Ace as he walked toward them. He snickered and shook his head. Never a dull moment when Anston Sharpe was around. Ace and

Colton shouldn't have worked. The two were as different as night and day, and yet somehow, they were perfect together. Not that Colton didn't have days where he also wanted to strangle his husband, but Ace always found a way to soothe Colton.

"Impeccable timing, as usual," Colton teased. He straightened and waited for Ace to reach him.

"Hey, sweetheart." Ace brought Colton into his arms for a kiss, one that required him to stretch a bit since Colton had a few inches on him. Despite Colton being almost six and a half feet tall, Ace had a way of projecting a bigger presence. As a former Green Beret, he was big and muscular, but his personality made him seem that much bigger. Rarely was the guy without a smile or smart aleck remark.

"So what's got you two so excited?" Ace asked.

"That." Colton motioned to Joshua's computer screen.

Stepping behind Joshua's desk, Ace peered over his shoulder. "Is that... a spreadsheet?" He threw Colton a questioning glance. "Are you two seriously drooling over a spreadsheet?"

Colton rolled his eyes. "It's not just a spreadsheet."

Joshua agreed. He thrust a hand toward the

screen. "Look at all the color coding! There's tabs, formulas, and hyperlinks. *Hyperlinks*, Ace. It's a masterpiece."

"Not gonna lie, I'm a little concerned right now." Ace studied the screen again. "Hold on." He leaned in. "Is this what I think it is?"

Joshua beamed brightly. "If I've learned anything in my time around the Kings, it's to always have a strategic, military-grade plan in place. I did all my research, compiled the data, entered it into my spreadsheet, and boom! *Joshua's Guide to Getting His Man* or *Operation Cuban Missile Conquest*. I'm still working on the title."

Ace stared at him for so long, Joshua worried he'd broken him. His lips twitched, and Joshua could tell he was trying hard not to lose it. "Did you just refer to his penis as a Cuban missile?"

"I absolutely did. What? You don't think my plan will work?"

"Not that I don't have faith in your man-obtaining mission, or your disturbingly detailed fact-gathering that I can safely assume Colton helped you with, it's more about the man all this"—Ace made a circling motion at the screen—"is for."

"What about him?"

"It's Frank."

Joshua peered at him. "Well, yeah. I thought you knew that." He moved his gaze to Colton, who looked amused for some reason. "I thought he knew that?"

"Of course I know," Ace said with a huff. "Everyone knows. My mother knows."

Wait, what? "How does your mother know?"

"That's not important. What I'm saying is that all your planning is great, and had it been any other guy, I dare say it might work, but we're talking about a man who frowns at puppies."

"He does not frown at puppies," Colton said with a laugh, playfully shoving Ace's shoulder.

"Fine. Maybe he doesn't, but when he does smile, it's very stern. I think I've seen him smile, like, a handful of times in the many years I've known him."

Colton shrugged. "He smiles at me all the time."

"And why is that?" Ace asked, eyes narrowed.

"Because he's my friend? Also, because I wanted to get into his pants when we first met."

Ace slapped a hand over his heart. "Ooh, ouch, right in the ventricle."

"You're ridiculous and I love you." Colton kissed Ace's cheek.

"I love you too. I can't blame Frank for smiling at you. You're gorgeous."

"Thank you, love. I'm not the only one Frank smiles at. He smiles at Joshua too."

"You're right. He's also forgotten how to people when he's around dear Joshua, which brings up my next point." Ace grinned knowingly at Joshua. "The two of you have a habit of short circuiting around each another. Your Cuban Missile Conquest calls for you to be able to form full sentences when speaking to him."

"True," Joshua admitted, turning in his chair to face them. "But that was before I realized he felt the same way I do about whatever's between us. For some reason, he keeps pulling away, and I want to know why."

Colton waved a hand in dismissal. "Oh, that part is easy."

Joshua's jaw dropped. He jumped to his feet, forcing Colton and Ace to scramble back so he wouldn't smack into them. "*What*? You've known this whole time and you didn't tell me?"

"I thought it was obvious."

"No, Colton. It was not obvious. At least not to me."

"Joshua, Frank is fourteen years older than you."

His expression softened. "He was out on the streets fending for himself before you were even born."

Joshua's argument died on his lips at the reminder of the hard life Frank had lived. How he'd been tossed out onto the street by his asshole parents when he'd been just a teen after accidentally being outed by his sister. Frank had been homeless for years, learning to survive as best he could on his own. Everyone knew Frank's story. It was the one piece of himself he'd shared with the world, because he needed everyone to know the importance of helping those who were in the same place he'd once been. Frank was a fighter and a protector.

"Frank has spent the majority of his life taking care of others, but who's taking care of *him*?"

Colton opened his mouth, and Joshua put a hand up to stop him. "I know what you're going to say. Frank doesn't believe he needs anyone to take care of him, because he's always taken care of himself. I want to show him that it's okay for him to lean on someone else. That after all this time of having to bear the weight of the world on his broad, sexy shoulders, I'm here to help bear some of that weight for him."

"Are you sure?" Colton asked gently. "Frank comes with a lot of baggage. He's not going to give up the fight that easy, especially when he thinks he's doing what's best for you."

"Then I'm simply going to have to show him that what he *thinks* is best for me isn't what *I* think is best for me." Joshua shook his head. "I can be just as stubborn."

Ace grinned wide and slapped his hands together to rub them gleefully. "This is going to be fun."

"You're terrible." Colton shook his head. "All right. Let us know how we can help."

"Thanks, Colton. Step one is infiltration. I need to find a way to spend more time with him. If I can figure out how—"

Ace's phone rang. "Hold that thought." He answered, and the dark expression that came onto his face was not a good sign. "I'm on my way." Hanging up, he kissed Colton. "I gotta go. The police just raided Sapphire Sands. Mason's there." Ace headed for the door, and Colton hurried after him.

"We're going with you."

Joshua darted over to Colton's side.

"Babe—" One arched eyebrow from Colton and Ace sighed. "Fine. But he's gonna be pissed, so approach with caution."

Thankfully, they were still at the office, which

meant they were a little closer to St. Augustine than Colton and Ace's mansion in Ponte Vedra. Still, it took Joshua a little under forty minutes to get there. Patrol cars lined the street outside the sleek black building, the neon Sapphire Sands sign casting a glow in the club's signature blue. Next to the club's name was a martini glass tipping to one side filled with glittering blue sand and on the glass's edge a blue hummingbird. One of these days, Joshua would have to remember to ask Frank about the significance of the hummingbird. No one seemed to know.

They went in through the back, let in by two huge security guards, both provided by Four Kings Security. Joshua had never been inside the club while it was closed. Instead of atmospheric lighting and a crowded dance floor packed with sweaty men enjoying themselves and getting intimate to an energetic beat, the house lights were on, the dance floor was empty, and tension filled the air as the staff huddled by the bar and the club members crowded to one side of the floor, as far away from the police as possible.

"Poor Frank," Joshua murmured as Ace went off to join Mason, Frank, and a blond man in an expensive suit who was attempting to keep Frank calm. Joshua would hazard a guess that was Frank's lawyer.

Sapphire Sands had a reputation, one Frank had carefully constructed for his club over the years. He'd built his empire with hard work, integrity, and a certain amount of ruthlessness. Bars and clubs closed around him, but Sapphire Sands continued to thrive because it provided an unrivaled service.

As a members-only nightclub and bar that catered to gay men of wealth and clout, Frank offered something in his establishment few could— safety, anonymity, and complete discretion. His client list was protected by the best security in the country, thanks to Four Kings Security's cyber security department.

Every client of Sapphire Sands was personally vetted by Frank himself and by Four Kings Security. All clients and staff members signed a non-disclosure agreement as part of their contract, one that came with a list of rules that were non-negotiable, and Joshua would know, seeing as how he signed one of those contracts when Frank offered him membership the first day they'd met.

"This has to be a terrible misunderstanding," Colton said quietly, shaking his head. "Everyone knows the rules, and nothing happens in this club without Frank knowing about it."

Anyone who broke one of Frank's rules was out on their ass, membership revoked, no second chances. Joshua had personally seen Frank revoke more than one membership.

Joshua's former boss had brought him to Sapphire Sands under false pretenses. As a client, his boss had applied for a one-time guest pass for Joshua, who'd been dragged into one of the back rooms where his asshole boss had hoped to fuck him. Joshua managed to get away and ended up in the bathroom, where he'd first met Colton. He'd been a mess, his clothes in disarray, eyes red and stinging from tears after he'd been fired for not letting the boss screw him.

Colton had walked in and been so kind, asking how he could help. They'd talked, and somehow Joshua ended up with a job offer to work at one of the most prestigious shipping companies in the country. He'd also met the man of his dreams, right before the man of his dreams kicked Joshua's old boss to the curb and revoked his membership. In that moment, Frank Ramirez became Joshua's knight in tarnished armor.

Of course, said knight had been doing his

damned best to keep his distance—despite the obvious heat between them—due to some misguided sense of duty.

Catching Seth's eye, Colton discreetly called him over. The three of them moved away from the staff to speak quietly.

"What's going on, Seth?" Colton asked.

"They're saying a club member came forward after witnessing the sale of drugs in the club."

"That's bullshit," Joshua hissed. Everyone knew the rules. Nothing happened in the club without consent. There was no illegal activity and no drugs of any kind. Club security was provided by the Kings, their surveillance top-of-the-line. Frank even had security officers in plain clothes to make sure no one broke the rules. "Who would be stupid enough to bring drugs into Frank's club?"

"There's always stupid," Seth muttered. "How many memberships has Frank revoked over the years because some rich asshole thinks the rules don't apply to him?"

"You think someone's messing with Frank?" Colton asked, his concern evident.

Seth let out a heavy sigh. "I wouldn't be surprised. You don't get to be in a position like Frank's without making enemies. Just because he plays fair doesn't mean everyone else does. Anyway, they have a warrant to search the club. Detective Asshole is demanding the client list, but that wasn't included in the search warrant, so without a new warrant that specifically names the client list, no way in hell will Frank give that up. King is looking into who made the allegation and the judge who signed the warrant. None of them seemed familiar with this judge, not even Mason."

Considering Mason had been part of the St. Augustine police force before being hired by Four Kings Security, that didn't bode well, but hearing that King was on the job offered some relief. Ward Kingston was a force to be reckoned with, and heaven help the poor bastard who hurt someone he cared about. The guy had flown to another *country* to hunt down a man who'd hurt one of his own. The asshole was serving life in a federal prison somewhere.

Four hours later, the police finished their search and found nothing. No trace of drugs or drug use, and they'd been thorough. Detective Asshole was *pissed*, but not as pissed as Frank, who decided for the security of his clients to close the club until Monday in the hopes the Kings and Mason would get to the bottom of this.

After talking to his clients and reassuring them, Frank sent them home, thanked Mason, sent his staff home—with the exception of Seth and Kit—then headed for his office. Joshua followed Ace and Colton as they trailed after Frank, the two of them quietly talking as they went.

Inside Frank's office, Frank whirled to face Ace and exploded. "I want to know who this son of a bitch is! Someone is fucking with me, with my reputation, my business. I want to know who I'm at war with."

"We'll find out who did this, Frank, but you need to—"

"Don't you fucking say it, Sharpe. If one more person tells me to calm down—"

"Frank?"

Frank stilled. He turned, his thick dark brows drawn together as if he'd only just realized Joshua was there, which was likely the case.

"Joshua?"

Without a second thought, Joshua crossed the room and gently placed a hand on Frank's arm. "It's going to be okay. The guys will get to the bottom of this. In the meantime, how can I help?"

Frank's shoulders dropped, and he appeared to

deflate, his anger seeming to leave with his heavy exhale. "Thanks, sweetheart, but I'm good."

"He's *not* good," Seth said, ignoring Frank's glare. "We hired an event manager because ours is on his honeymoon. The event company we've been using for years disappeared off the face of the freaking earth, and the new one we hired is doing fuck all, but they were the only ones available on such short notice. The first event manager they sent was an ass who showed up once, then never returned, and they haven't sent a replacement. I'm doing the best I can, but I don't know anything about hosting events, much less one of this scale, which means Frank and I have been working seven days a week trying to make this happen. We had a burst pipe in the employee lounge that's being fixed, and now a PR nightmare to face. We need help."

"Damn it, Seth," Frank growled.

"Stop being a stubborn ass. We need help. I want to go home and sleep with my boyfriend, and you just need to sleep. Period."

Joshua took hold of Frank's chin and turned his face so their gazes could meet. Standing this close, Joshua was stunned by the dark circles around Frank's usually bright eyes. "When was the last time you slept?"

"Thirty-two hours," Seth grumbled.

Joshua gasped. "*What?*"

"Did you forget I pay your salary?" Frank barked at Seth, who didn't look the least bit intimidated. Poor Kit looked worriedly from his boyfriend to Frank.

"Did you forget I don't give a fuck?"

"Asshole."

"Right back at ya." Seth folded his arms over his expansive chest and waited for Frank to push back on this, but he didn't. He just grumbled at Seth.

"Let me help you." Joshua laid his palms on Frank's chest, getting his attention. Their gazes met, those intense honey-colored eyes making it easy for Joshua to lose himself. In that moment he saw it, something he'd never seen in Frank before tonight. Joshua doubted Frank had ever let his guard down long enough for anyone to see it.

Vulnerability.

Frank Ramirez was an intimidating man familiar with the shadows. It was evident in the way he moved, in the confidence he exuded. He was reserved and respected, but as he placed his hands on Joshua's and squeezed, he let Joshua see a tiny part of himself that few, if any, had probably seen.

The stubble had grown in thick and dark,

matching his thick black eyebrows and the soft waves of his hair. It was getting long, curling around the backs of his ears, a strand escaping to fall over his brow. He was as imposing as ever, dressed in his signature black suit, shirt, and tie, his shoulders impossibly wide.

"Let me help," Joshua said again.

"You already have a job."

"True," Colton pitched in from beside Ace.

Seeming to realize they weren't alone, Frank tenderly moved Joshua's hands off his chest. Joshua dropped his arms, but he didn't leave Frank's side.

"Joshua does have a job," Colton continued. "But he's also been training someone to fill in for him for when he's out of the office. This would be a perfect opportunity for them to step up. Plus, Joshua has time off he needs to take."

Frank shook his head. "It's too much."

Ace snickered. "Frank, Joshua managed both Colton's work *and* wedding schedule. Pretty sure he can handle anything at this point."

"I can attest to that. He impressed Leo's father, and he's a retired Army general." Colton came to stand next to Frank and put a hand on his shoulder.

"Let Joshua help you."

Joshua waited with bated breath as Frank thought about it.

Exhaustion must have taken over, because Frank gave in. "Okay. Thank you."

"Perfect," Joshua said cheerfully. "First things first. Let's go to bed."

THREE

THIS WAS A HUGE MISTAKE.

As much as Frank appreciated his friends wanting to help, he wasn't oblivious. Colton was one of Frank's closest friends. He was also a meddler. Ace was just as bad. Good thing Fitz hadn't shown up, or Frank would have been faced with the trifecta of matchmaking menaces.

Instead, he faced a far greater threat.

Joshua Sterling was in his early thirties, fair-haired, with big blue-green eyes and a sinful body that fit perfectly against Frank's. That knowledge was something he could have done without, but not only had Joshua ended up pressed against him once, but *twice*. Once clothed, the second during a day at the beach when he'd been volunteered by his meddling friends to swim Joshua out to the sandbar after Joshua admitted he couldn't swim in water that was too deep for his feet to touch the bottom. Their wet bodies pressed together in the hot sun had been torture, but Frank had survived.

For months, Frank had managed to keep his distance from the beautiful young man, and now to complete the fuckery that was his life, Joshua stood in front of him, the words *"Let's go to bed,"* having just come from between his plump lips.

Clearly, he hadn't meant for *them* to go to bed, but still, not something Frank needed to hear while the man he'd been dreaming of since they'd met stood so close.

"Right." Eloquent, he was not. Frank motioned to the door.

"What time do you want me here?"

"Since we're going to be closed for the weekend, we can catch up on some of the event stuff. How about five?"

"Sure. I'll grab us some coffees on the way here. I'll text you and you can tell me what kind."

"Coffee?"

"Yeah, I don't function that early in the morning without it."

"Morning?" Frank almost tripped over his own

feet on the way to the door. "Jesus Christ, what the hell are you doing waking up at five in the morning?"

Joshua blinked at him. "Um, getting ready for work?"

Frank glared at Colton, who laughed.

"What? Don't look at me like that. We work office jobs. We start at eight."

"That's terrifying." Frank yawned as he led everyone out into the hall.

"Go on," Seth said. "I'll lock up and set the alarm."

Frank rubbed his eyes. Normally he would have taken care of it himself, but now his body knew sleep was near, it was shutting down on him. "Okay. Thank you, Seth."

"You're welcome," Seth replied, patting him on the back. "You're also about to get pissed at me again." He turned to the guys. "Can someone give him a ride home?"

"I can drive myself." Yawning through his growl did nothing to help his case. He didn't bother arguing. The look Seth gave him said it wasn't up for discussion. That's what he got for having friends. Pains in the ass. Frank tossed his car keys to Seth.

"I'll take him," Joshua said, his smile sweet.

Perfect.

Well, if he was going to work with Joshua, he might as well get used to being in close proximity to him. No, this was good. The two of them working close together would prove how unsuited they were for each other. Maybe once Joshua got a good look at what a miserable fuck he was, he'd get the idea of them as something more out of his head.

They headed out into the parking lot behind the club, where they said their goodbyes. Only four cars remained in the lot: Seth's blue Dodge Charger, Ace's red Corvette Stingray Coupe 3LT—a Christmas present from his husband—Frank's black Audi R8 Coupe, and...

"You drive an SUV?" Frank stood next to the small black Nissan.

Joshua blinked at him. "Yeah. Why?"

"I pictured you driving something a little flashier." He opened the passenger door and climbed in. The guys Frank knew who were Joshua's age and earned what he did as *the* top executive assistant for Connolly Maritime would have gone out and splurged on a luxury car the first chance they got.

Joshua pressed the ignition button to start the car. "I love this car. It's got the three P's."

"What's that?"

"Pretty, practical, and paid off. Sure, I *could*

upgrade now that I got rid of my student debt, but I don't really need a new car. Why spend all that money? A car's just something to get you from point A to point B."

"Ever drive an Audi?"

"Nope." Joshua motioned out the window at Frank's car. "I'm guessing that's yours. Looks pricey." He handed his phone to Frank, the GPS app open.

Frank didn't think twice about entering his home address. "Two hundred."

Some kind of weird gasp/squeak came out of Joshua. "Two hundred *thousand* dollars?"

"Yes." Frank returned his phone to him. He held back a smile as Joshua absently took the phone and connected it to his car, the GPS map popping up on the dashboard screen. "You okay?"

"Yeah, I need a second for my brain to reboot. Okay."

Frank chuckled. He really was too cute.

"And you're just going to leave it in the parking lot?" Joshua asked, incredulous.

"What? Of course not. I gave my car keys to Seth. Kit will drive Seth's car home, and Seth will take mine. He'll pick me up on the way to work tomorrow. I'll let you drive the Audi sometime. Then you can tell me if you still believe a car is just something to get you from point A to point B."

"You'd let me drive your car?"

"Sure."

"Why?"

Hm, good question. Frank shrugged. "I trust you."

"You don't really know me." Joshua pulled out of the parking lot and into the quiet street.

"We've sort of known each other for almost three years." Not that they'd spent a whole lot of time together, and whatever time they *had* spent together was with Colton, the Kings, and their boyfriends.

"I suppose you're right."

"Also, I'm an excellent judge of character."

Joshua's expression turned wicked. "And yet you give Ace full access to your club."

Frank laughed. "Maybe not that good a judge."

They both snickered, and Frank felt himself relax. He'd expected a lot of awkwardness at being alone with Joshua. Not that there weren't awkward moments between them, but they seemed to be getting better at communicating. What had changed? He snuck a glance at Joshua, his heart skipping a beat at the soft smile on Joshua's face.

A somewhat familiar song Frank couldn't place floated quietly up from the speakers.

"What are you listening to right now?"

Joshua's eyes went huge, and he slowly moved his thumb on the steering wheel to press a button. The music turned off. "Nothing."

"Now I'm really intrigued."

Joshua let out a groan. "Savage Garden. When I was eight years old, I was obsessed with that album. I played the CD so much it got scratched to hell and my mom had to buy me another one."

"Eight years old?" Frank winced. Christ, he'd been graduating from college at the time.

"What were *you* listening to?"

"Not Savage Garden."

Joshua snorted. "Given. So, what were you listening to?"

"Nirvana. Pearl Jam. Alice in Chains. Yep. I embraced the whole grunge thing." The delight on Joshua's face made Frank smile.

"Oh my God, no you did not."

"I did. My hair was long, I wore eyeliner, torn jeans, baggy T-shirts with a plaid shirt tied around my waist. I had two earrings, one on my left eyebrow, the other in my left ear."

Joshua shook his head. "My mind is blown right

now, just…" He made an explosion sound to go with his hand motion.

The shock was understandable. Like everyone else in Frank's life, Joshua knew him as the man he was now, not the lost youth trying to find his place in the world that he'd once been. After college, he left his past and everyone in it behind to start over in St. Augustine. He'd never looked back.

"Thanks for driving me," Frank murmured, rubbing his eyes again. "I really would have been okay."

"Better safe than sorry."

Frank couldn't argue with that. It wasn't until he startled awake that he even realized he'd fallen asleep. How long had Joshua been parked outside his house? "Shit. Sorry."

"For what? Falling asleep after being up a ridiculous number of hours? It's okay. Get some sleep. I'll see you tomorrow."

"See you tomorrow, and, um, thanks for the help. Hopefully you won't regret it."

Joshua frowned. "Why would I regret it?"

"I've been known to be a bit of an asshole."

"Hm. We'll see."

Frank got out and closed the door behind him. He had no reason to stop and look back, but he did.

Joshua waved cheerfully at him, his boyish smile wide. They could do this. Joshua was a friend helping him out, that's all. Frank waved at him, then went inside. Tomorrow would be a day like any other. He could handle this. Everything would be just fine.

EVERYTHING WAS NOT FINE.

Lifting his gaze over the monitor, Frank studied Joshua, dressed smartly in navy pants and a gray knit sweater over a white shirt and black tie. He stood in front of the costume rack, absently running a hand over one of the feather boas while he spoke to the event company over the phone. For once, Frank didn't care about the growing pile of blue feathers on his carpet.

Frank had arrived at the club just before five and found Joshua already there, leaning against the wall next to the back door, phone in hand as the wind rustled his hair. He'd lifted his head, met Frank's gaze, and the dazzling smile that spread across his beautiful face stole Frank's breath away. What had Frank done? He'd managed a grunt in greeting, slid open the panel to the high-tech lock, and failed to enter the correct alarm code. Twice. Thankfully, he hadn't been able to screw up the retina and thumb scan.

Hoping to get his shit together, he gave Joshua a tour of the club and back of house area, pointed out where everything was in his office since that's where Joshua would be working, and got him connected to the office's secure Wi-Fi. That had been an hour ago.

Joshua had come a long way from the scared, uncertain young man he'd been when they'd first met. Then again, a lot had been going wrong for Joshua that day. From the moment Frank laid eyes on him, he'd felt a fierce sense of protectiveness, and he hadn't hesitated in coming to Joshua's aid. More importantly, Joshua had felt safe with Frank, walking straight into his embrace when he'd offered comfort.

Working for Colton appeared to have helped Joshua restore his confidence. He was sweet and polite as he addressed the owner of the event company, detailing exactly what he expected from them and when. His voice never rose, and he remained calm the entire time, chatting as if they were old friends. Frank stared in awe.

"I'm so excited to be helping Frank. When my boss heard what was going on, he loaned me out to help. The two are such good friends. Who's my boss?

Colton Connolly, of Connolly Maritime. Yes, the billionaire." Joshua chuckled. "Oh my gosh, the wedding was stunning. Obscenely expensive, but beautiful. Did you know both Colton and his husband had their bachelor parties at Sapphire Sands?"

As if feeling Frank's gaze on him, Joshua glanced over, and the little shit winked at him. He actually winked. At Frank. Not entirely sure what to do with that, Frank turned his attention back to his monitor and the employee schedule he'd done nothing with for the last half hour.

"Thank you so much, Alma. I appreciate it. Yes, of course. We look forward to working with you. Talk to you soon." Joshua hung up and tapped away at his phone, then slipped it into his pocket. "Neema, your new event manager, will be here tonight at eight. Before she arrives, you'll receive an email containing a link and log-in details to a client portal where you'll find the customized theme package she's putting together for you. It'll contain 3D renderings for the winter theme you picked, the decorations needed for each setup, and budget estimates. Once the theme and decor are confirmed, Neema will go through catering options with you, menu options, update the renderings with the planned layout of tables, chairs, stages, centerpieces, and so on. The dancers will be here tomorrow at two. I've already texted Kit to let him know."

Frank stared at Joshua. He opened his mouth, but no words came out. With a smile, Joshua removed his phone from his pocket.

"Also, I've pulled up several restaurants in the area with excellent reviews that offer both dine-in and delivery options for dinner. What are you in the mood for?"

That was a loaded question if he ever heard one. What he was in the mood for was Joshua, naked, with Frank balls-deep in his ass. Fuck dinner. He wanted dessert. Ooh, this was such a bad idea.

"You choose. But we're dining out," Frank grumbled, standing. A busy restaurant would ensure he kept his hands to himself.

Joshua stopped in front of him. "You have something, um…" He reached out and swiped his thumb over the corner of Frank's bottom lip. His lips twitched like he wanted to smile. "Glitter?"

"Unfortunate snowman incident."

Joshua eyed him, like he wasn't sure if Frank was messing with him or not. "I would really like to hear about this incident."

"Never gonna happen."

"Now I want to hear about it even more."

"No."

Joshua nodded, his smile wide. "It needs to happen."

"I admire your determination, but it's not happening."

"Hm." Joshua dropped his gaze to Frank's mouth. "We'll see." His low, sultry voice promised things Frank had no business even thinking about. He barely stifled a groan before Joshua informed him, "You're driving."

"So bossy." Frank leaned in ever so slightly when he caught a whiff of the familiar scent. "Ambre Nuit by Christian Dior."

"My favorite." Joshua's sexy purr sent a shiver through Frank. "You gave it to me for Christmas, remember?"

Frank tilted his head. "I didn't know it was your favorite."

"You're adorable." Joshua ran a finger down Frank's tie. "It's my favorite because you gave it to me."

Well, shit. "We should go." Frank turned, glowering at Seth, who stood in the doorway looking amused. "Why don't you go ahead. I'll catch up. I need to talk to Seth a minute."

"Sure." Joshua grabbed his jacket, and as soon as he was gone, Frank snatched up his own jacket and stopped in front of Seth.

"How long have you been standing there?"

"Long enough to know you need to marry that man," Seth said cheerfully.

Frank sighed. "There's nothing going on between us, and there won't be."

"Why? He's a great guy, and there's obviously a strong connection between the two of you."

"He's young."

Seth gave him a pointed look. "So are you." He sighed at Frank's glower and stepped to one side. "The only one who has an issue with his age is you. Joshua doesn't care. I don't care. None of your friends care. Hell, look at King and Leo. You don't see King hung up on Leo's age."

"Leo is different."

"Well, yeah," Seth agreed, smiling. "But still."

"I have to go." Frank headed down the hall, calling out over his shoulder. "We'll be back before the event manager arrives."

"Okay. Just think about it, Frank."

It seemed like all he did was think about it. The truth of the matter was, Joshua's age wasn't as big a deal to him as his friends thought. Plenty of gay men his age dated younger men. The age gap was one of several reasons why they wouldn't work, the biggest strike against him being the fact that he was already in a committed relationship.

Sapphire Sands had come between him and more than one man he'd made the mistake of caring about, men who in the beginning assured him they had no problem with his work life. Not that he ever blamed them for breaking things off, but each time he fooled himself into thinking it would be different, he'd once again find himself alone. The arguments had been the worst. Accusations of infidelity, because why else would he be at his club all night, surrounded by horny wealthy men if it wasn't to fuck them?

With a heavy sigh, he shook those grim thoughts from his head. He'd taken a lot of risks in his lifetime, carrying the scars of his losses. He couldn't bear the thought of adding Joshua to that list, which was why nothing could or would happen between them.

FOUR

"I'M SO SORRY."

Joshua waved a hand in dismissal. "It's fine, Frank. Stop apologizing." As disappointing as it was, Joshua understood completely, something he'd been trying to convince Frank of since the restaurant. There was no need for him to keep apologizing.

Dinner at the amazing little Italian restaurant down the street turned into takeout. Their food had just arrived when Frank received a call from Seth. Clients were cancelling their Winterland reservations, thanks to the raid on the club. Frank had apologized to Joshua and asked the waiter to box up their food. Less than fifteen minutes later they were back at Sapphire Sands.

"I need to make some phone calls," Frank said as

he made his way toward the back of house area. "Can you deal with the event manager if I'm not done by the time she arrives?"

"Of course."

Seth waited for them by Frank's office door. He smiled apologetically at Joshua, then turned to Frank. "I think we can turn this around and ease their minds. Jack called. He and his cyber security team have been on the case, and they're onto something, but Jack has a couple of questions for you before he confirms."

"Thanks, Seth." Frank stopped to face Joshua. "Why don't you go ahead and enjoy your dinner. I'll be out as soon as I can."

"Okay. Let me know if you need me."

"Thank you." Frank was about to walk off when Joshua caught his arm. He held one of the bags of food out.

"Make sure you eat something."

Frank's expression softened. "Thanks, sweetheart." He kissed Joshua's cheek like it was the most natural thing in the world and took the bag of food from him.

What just happened? Joshua blinked up at him, but Frank seemed oblivious as he headed into his office.

No big deal. It was only a peck on the cheek, right? Shaking himself out of it, Joshua turned and almost bumped into Seth, who stood gaping.

"What?"

"Nothing, it's just..." Seth leaned in to murmur quietly, "Frank's not a PDA kind of guy, especially at the club. When he's here, he's usually all business."

"Oh well. I'm sure he didn't even realize he did it. He's got a lot on his mind right now."

Seth hummed, his lips quirked at the corner. "You're probably right. I better go. Make yourself at home."

"Thanks." As much as Joshua wanted to do a little happy dance at the thought, he refrained from letting himself get excited. Chances were Frank wouldn't even remember having kissed his cheek.

Feeling a bit weird about having his dinner in the employee lounge, or at least the staging area that was serving as the employee lounge, Joshua carried his food out into the club and scanned the floor. Feeling a little naughty, he hurried excitedly over to one of the VIP sections.

On special occasions when the Kings had something to celebrate, they'd come to Sapphire Sands, and the times Joshua had been with them, they'd been seated in one of the VIP sections. Joshua had never been a VIP of anything. His talent in cat wrangling had always been appreciated and at times coveted, because he had a knack for knowing what people needed, but he'd always been the background guy. Behind every great person was an often uncredited and underappreciated assistant.

Not that Joshua expected any credit for doing his job, but until Colton, no other boss had acknowledged Joshua's worth. As an executive assistant, his job was to keep his boss's life running as smoothly as possible, both personally and professionally. He loved what he did, and for the first time ever, he wasn't on the outside looking in.

Sitting at the huge table and taking in the club around him, Joshua couldn't help but do a happy little shimmy. He loved being helpful, and he loved even more knowing he was able to help Frank in some way. As he ate his incredible meal, he brought his spreadsheet up on his phone. It was over-the-top and ridiculous, but Frank wasn't like the others. Something deep inside Joshua told him Frank was *the* one. The least he could do was try, and if his best wasn't good enough, then, well, what else could he do but accept that Frank didn't want him.

Pushing that thought aside, Joshua dove into his

dinner. He *loved* carbonara, and this one was particularly amazing. Maybe he'd suggest they go back for dinner one night. He'd just finished cleaning up after himself when something shimmery caught his eye. Maybe someone had dropped something. Crossing the floor, he crouched down and put his finger to the sparkling white. Was this... glitter? Why was there white glitter on the floor? He remembered the matching speck he'd wiped off Frank's lip. He *really* needed to find out about this snowman incident.

The club's front doorbell went off, and he quickly wiped his hand on his pants, then hurried over. A petite woman dressed in a charcoal gray pantsuit and gorgeous dark curls smiled brightly at him. He returned her smile and unlocked the door to let her in.

"Neema?"

"Yes, and you must be Joshua.."

"It's so great to meet you." Joshua took her outstretched hand and shook it. "How did you know I wasn't Frank?"

Her hazel eyes sparkled with amusement. "Let's just say my predecessor was more than a little intimidated by Mr. Ramirez, and although I'm sure you can be intimidating, you're not quite scary enough to have my colleague questioning his life choices."

"And you're still here after that glowing reference?" Joshua teased.

"Honey, Frank Ramirez doesn't scare me. I have three teenage daughters and a Chihuahua named Hannibal."

Joshua snickered. "Oh, I like you. I think you and Frank will get along fine." The back doors swung open and Frank emerged, all broad shoulders, black shirt sleeves rolled up to his elbows to expose his corded forearms. His tie was gone, the top two buttons of his shirt undone, and his hair tousled from where he'd clearly been running his fingers through it.

"Sweet heaven," Neema murmured.

"Yeah, he has that effect on people." The sigh couldn't be helped.

Neema smiled knowingly at him. "I bet."

Joshua was pleasantly surprised when Frank stopped in front of him and put a hand to Joshua's lower back.

"You have a good dinner?"

"It was amazing. Thank you."

"I'm glad to hear it." He turned to Neema and

held a hand out. "You must be Neema. I'm Frank, and you've already met Joshua."

"A pleasure to meet you, and yes, Joshua and I have met."

"Great. Why don't we set up out here? My office is a little crowded at the moment with the employee lounge currently undergoing repairs." He motioned to the same table Joshua had sat at to have his dinner. Did Frank know that? The little smirk he threw Joshua's way said he did, and it made Joshua's heart skip a beat. First a kiss on the cheek, now a wicked little smile? The man was trying to kill him.

They spent the next several hours going through the entire event package Neema had organized, everything from centerpieces and table settings to menus and entertainment. It was exciting, seeing Frank's vision come together. Joshua had been more than a little surprised when Frank asked his opinion on several design choices, and even more surprised when Frank agreed with his choices. It had been fun.

There was still a lot to do and coordinate, but their meeting with Neema had gone exceptionally well. Some of the tension had eased from Frank's shoulders now that orders had been confirmed. It was close to midnight by the time they were ready to go home.

"I've just gotta put a few things away in the office and lock up. Then we can head out together," Frank said.

"Sure thing."

While Frank went to finish up, Joshua decided to wander the club. It took Frank a good fifteen to twenty minutes to lock up the back end of the club before he was ready to turn the lights off and set the alarm. Now that he thought about it, Frank had given him a tour of the club, but he'd only motioned toward the back rooms. He hadn't actually taken Joshua back there.

Curious, Joshua stepped through a set of thick black curtains that led to a narrow hall with rows of curtained-off sections to each side. Beyond the curtained-off sections were rooms, the black doors only visible against the black walls because of the strips of neon across the top of the doorways in the club's signature blue.

Joshua had never been in one of these rooms with anyone. He'd certainly not gotten up to anything. The times he'd visited the club, he'd seen the Kings and their significant others disappear into the back rooms at one point or another.

The doors to the rooms were all open since they were unoccupied, and Joshua walked into the first one. The black room was just big enough for its intended purpose, with a tufted black velvet couch against the wall and a trash can beside it. A small, high-black table contained a silver tray of wet wipes, and in front of the couch sat a black coffee table with a bowl of condoms and lube in the center. The place was spotless. Considering how Frank felt about his club, Joshua wasn't surprised. He'd have to ask Frank how he managed that.

"I'll just sample one of these, if you don't mind," Joshua said to no one in particular as he pocketed one of the condoms and a packet of lube.

Knowing what these rooms were used for had his overactive imagination conjuring up all manner of sinfully sexy scenarios. Instead of random half-naked sweaty men in suits, one particular suited man came to mind.

What would it be like to have Frank hold him up against the wall, kiss the breath out of him, fuck him fast and hard? With a moan, Joshua fell back against the wall. He closed his eyes, willing himself to calm down. This was bad. He shouldn't be in here. He definitely shouldn't be in here thinking about Frank fucking him, sinking slowly into him until he was balls-deep. Frank's heavier weight against him would feel so damned good, and when he moved...

"Joshua?"

Frank's low rumble made Joshua groan, until he realized that voice had come from *outside* of his head. He opened his eyes and glanced over at the door where Frank stood, his gasp caught in his throat at the heat in Frank's eyes.

"Hi." Joshua's voice came out low and throaty. He turned toward the door, his side pressed against the wall as he took in every inch of the gorgeous man.

"What, um... what are you doing in here?" Frank asked, taking a tentative step inside the room.

"I've never been in here with anyone."

"I know."

Joshua's head shot up and he met Frank's gaze. Had Frank been watching him? How else would he know Joshua had never accompanied anyone into the back rooms?

"I was curious. When I stepped inside, I started thinking..." Joshua stayed where he was. If Frank wanted to do something about whatever had him looking at Joshua the way he was, like he wanted to fuck him into submission, then he'd have to make the first move. That didn't mean Joshua couldn't help him along.

Frank took a step closer. "What were you thinking?"

"Of you fucking me." He held Frank's gaze. "Up against the wall." Joshua's cock strained against his pants as Frank let out a low feral growl.

"Is that what you want? To be fucked in some club's back room?"

Joshua left the wall and stopped in front of Frank. He placed a hand on Frank's chest as he gazed up at him.

"Sapphire Sands isn't just some club where men go to fuck. It's a home, a safe space. Somewhere they can be themselves and forget about the world outside. You did that, Frank. You built a community, one that helps others. So no, I don't want to be fucked in some club's back room. I want to be fucked here, in a place that means something to you."

"You're amazing, you know that?" Frank's smile stole Joshua's breath away, right before his mouth on Joshua's finished the job.

An inferno of need erupted through Joshua as he met Frank's ravenous hunger with his own. Never had he been kissed with such fire and passion. Joshua curled his fingers around the lapels of Frank's suit jacket, whether to hold himself up or to keep Frank close, he had no idea, but the longer Frank kissed him, the more Joshua needed.

Frank's tongue tangled with his, the heat of his

mouth, the feel of his lips, and his strong arms wrapped around Joshua fueled the flames raging inside him. Just as he'd fantasized, Frank pushed him up against the wall, his lips tearing away from Joshua's to suck at his neck, then ear.

"Oh God," Joshua moaned, his head thrown back as Frank kissed and nibbled his neck. Joshua slipped his hand lower, cupping Frank in his slacks, his groan joining Frank's as he palmed that big, hard cock. "I want this inside me so bad," Joshua said, his voice hoarse and raspy. "Please, Frank."

Frank made quick work of their belts, unfastening and unzipping. Their pants dropped to the floor, and Joshua let go of Frank long enough to toe off his shoes and grab the supplies he'd stuck in his pocket earlier. He stepped out of his pants and shoved his boxer-briefs down. Something about seeing Frank still dressed in his suit with his leaking cock jutted up toward his stomach made Joshua weak in the knees.

"You're so damned sexy," Joshua murmured, handing the supplies to Frank with one hand and wrapping the other around Frank's cock. He ran his thumb over the pearls of precome, using it to ease the friction as he stroked Frank, their mouths reunited. Frank palmed Joshua's asscheeks, kneading the globes before he hauled Joshua off his feet. Not expecting the sudden movement, Joshua flailed and threw his arms around Frank's neck.

"Easy," Frank said through a chuckle. "I got you."

Joshua snorted. "Of course you do. Your muscles are obscene." He nipped at Frank's stubbled jaw and wrapped his legs around Frank's waist as he was held against the wall. "And I want to lick each and every one of them. But first, I want you buried deep in my ass."

"Fuck. The things that come out of your mouth," Frank said through a moan.

"Aren't as exciting as the things I want to go in it."

"You're going to be a handful, aren't you?"

"You up for the challenge?" Joshua ran his tongue over Frank's bottom lip and squeezed his cock, loving the way Frank's eyes all but rolled into the back of his head. "I'm going to take that as a yes."

Frank claimed Joshua's mouth, kissing the breath out of him. Joshua was so hard, he ached. If Frank didn't fuck him right now, he was going to lose his mind.

"Frank, *now*."

"So bossy," Frank growled, the smile clear in his eyes. "I kinda like it. Let's not waste any time, then."

FIVE

SO MUCH FOR nothing happening between them.

Frank should have known better. The more time he spent around Joshua, the harder it was to keep his distance. When he'd searched for Joshua, the last place he'd expected to find him was in one of the back rooms. All kinds of sinful scenarios had played out in his head, but when Joshua said he wanted Frank to fuck him in the club because of what it meant to him, he'd been done.

And then they'd kissed.

Joshua was unlike anyone he'd ever met—always smiling, cheerful, eager to help. He was attentive and caring, beautiful inside and out. And for some reason, he wanted Frank.

"Frank, please."

How the hell could he deny Joshua anything? Frank was so turned on he was in danger of coming before they'd even gotten started. Joshua's sinewy body fit perfectly against his, and Frank couldn't get enough of Joshua's mouth, of his taste. He held on to Joshua with one arm, pinning him against the wall with his body as he handed the lube packet to Joshua, then carefully tore the condom packet open with his teeth. With the condom rolled onto his rock-hard cock, he held his two fingers up to Joshua, their eyes meeting. A wicked smile spread across Joshua's face as he squeezed the lube onto Frank's fingers.

Joshua placed his lips next to Frank's ear and murmured silkily, "Fuck me with your fingers, Frank."

With a groan, Frank pressed his lubed fingers to Joshua's entrance and gently pushed in, his deep moan mixing with Joshua's as Frank's fingers were swallowed by that tight heat. Slowly at first, Frank moved his fingers until Joshua was rutting against him, his panting breath filling the quiet room.

"Frank," Joshua whispered, need and desperation in his voice. He gasped and threw back his head as Frank picked up his pace, pushing his fingers deep inside Joshua and pulling them out.

Frank's stomach tightened at the decadent noises from Joshua as he begged Frank to fuck him.

"Oh God, I need your cock inside me, Frank."

"Yeah?" Frank nipped at Joshua's chin.

"Yes!"

Removing his fingers, Frank replaced them with the tip of his cock. Joshua was all but trembling in his arms as Frank breached his hole, sinking slowly inside him.

"Fuck, you're so tight," Frank growled. And it felt so damned good.

Joshua writhed in Frank's arms, his moans and curses sweet music to Frank's ears as he started to move, gingerly pulling out almost to the tip before slowly sinking back inside.

"Couch," Joshua demanded, and Frank didn't so much as hesitate. He carried Joshua to the couch and sat down, his cock buried deep inside Joshua, who sat astride his lap.

"Oh fuck," Frank grabbed hold of Joshua's asscheeks and pumped himself inside him, their bodies smacking together in the silence of the room sounding deliciously erotic. Frank's body thrummed with need as Joshua took his pleasure from Frank, bouncing on him, driving Frank inside him over and over. Joshua's plump lips were parted, his hair plastered to his brow as he moved.

Frank changed his angle, and Joshua cried out. He took hold of Frank's shirt and tore it open, buttons popping off and pinging against the wall and side table.

"Jesus." Frank closed his eyes, his head thrown back as Joshua tweaked on of his nipples. He ran his hands over Frank's chest, down over the muscles of his abdomen.

"I want to come all over you, Frank." Joshua sloppily kissed him before moving his mouth to Frank's ear. "Mark you as mine. Will you let me?"

"Anything for you, baby." The scary thing was that he meant it. All Joshua had to do was ask and Frank would make it happen. No one had ever had that kind of power over him, and it terrified him.

"Stay with me, Frank," Joshua's plea was barely above a whisper as he cupped Frank's face. He peppered kisses over Frank's cheeks and nose, down his jawline, his movements slowing to match the tender gesture.

"I'm here," Frank replied quietly. He wrapped his arms around Joshua and slipped one hand under his shirt to slide up the curve of his spine. His skin was soft and warm, his presence soothing.

Passion fueled their kisses, but also tenderness and an affection that could quickly turn to something far deeper if they weren't careful. Did he want careful? Their bodies moved as one, Joshua's arms around Frank's neck and his lips on Frank's.

Frank snapping his hips had Joshua crying out his name as hot come hit Frank's abdomen, shoving him over the edge. He thrust several more times before his muscles tightened and his orgasm slammed into him. He buried his shout in Joshua's hair as he pumped a few more times before he was too sensitive to continue.

Their panting breaths was all that could be heard in the room, and Frank closed his eyes, a smile spreading across his face when Joshua snuggled into him with a contented sigh. Frank ran a soothing hand over Joshua's back and nuzzled his hair. He could get used to this, to having Joshua in his arms.

"Come home with me." The words were out of Frank's mouth before he could stop them. What the hell was he thinking? Obviously, he wasn't thinking at all. All his thinking being done for him by certain parts of his anatomy. He considered playing off the request, but Joshua sat back, his smile squeezing Frank's heart.

"Yeah?"

Frank was in so much trouble. He cupped Joshua's face and ran a thumb over his cheek. "Yes."

"I would love that." Joshua leaned in and brushed his lips over Frank's.

Kissing Joshua was quickly becoming Frank's favorite thing. The taste of him, the feel of his body against Frank's, the emotion and passion behind each kiss. Joshua wanted him as much as Frank wanted Joshua. It was evident in the way he looked at Frank, the way he smiled at him, touched him. Frank had never desired someone's touch like he did Joshua's. Everything about him was so... real.

"Oh my God," Joshua said through a gasp, his eyes huge. "I ripped your shirt. It was probably ridiculously expensive."

It was, but Joshua didn't need to know that. Frank waved a hand in dismissal. "It's fine. I've got plenty more shirts." He'd give up more than his expensive shirts to have Joshua. Plucking a few wipes from the side table, he kissed Joshua as he cleaned them up. He smiled at the slash of red that had appeared across Joshua's cheeks.

"Let's get out of here before I end up fucking you again."

"And that would be a bad thing?"

"No, but I'd rather have you in my bed."

"Let's go, then."

Frank chuckled as Joshua quickly got off him and rushed for his clothes. As soon as they were dressed, they hurried out into the club toward the back door. Thank fuck he didn't live far from the club. In less than half an hour, he was pulling into his garage. He got out and closed the garage door just as Joshua was out of the car. Turning off the house alarm, he unlocked the door and ushered Joshua inside.

The second the door closed behind them, they were stripping, clothes littering the floor as they kissed their way to Frank's bedroom, stopping only long enough to flip on some lights so they wouldn't trip over themselves. Thankfully, Frank managed to get them there without breaking anything. Good thing his bedroom wasn't on the second floor.

The back of Joshua's legs hit the mattress, and he fell back onto it. He stared at Frank, eyes wide.

"You okay?" Frank asked. Moonlight filtered in through the open blinds to cast a glow around Joshua —as if he wasn't already breathtaking. A slow nod was Joshua's response as he raked his gaze over every inch of Frank.

"And here I thought you couldn't get any sexier," Joshua murmured. "I was wrong. So very, very wrong." He ran his tongue over his bottom lip, a shiver going through him when Frank placed a knee on the bed. "How do you want me?"

"On your hands and knees."

Joshua whimpered, then quickly scrambled to do as Frank asked, the sight making Frank groan. He turned on the bedside lamp, then grabbed supplies. Climbing onto the bed, he positioned himself behind Joshua, a hand to his plump asscheek. Before this sweet, cheerful man appeared in his life, Frank had never had an issue with self-control. He'd been described as stoic and imposing, among other things, but never impulsive. And now? Now he found himself on his knees worshipping the beautiful young man in front of him.

"Frank," Joshua pleaded.

Frank answered Joshua's plea with a kiss to his lower back, right before he speared Joshua's hole with his tongue.

"Holy fuuuuck!" Joshua's body shook. He dropped to his elbows, his ass in the air and his head on his arms. The invitation sent a shiver through Frank. Inhaling deeply, he released a guttural moan.

"You smell so damned good." He didn't give Joshua time to reply, at least not with words. Spreading Joshua's cheeks, Frank set out to wreck him, to turn him into a pleading, writhing mess. He wrapped a hand around Joshua's stiff cock as he licked, nipped, and laved at his entrance, alternating between using his tongue and his fingers until Joshua was on the brink of coming. Pulling at Joshua's thighs, he smiled at the little grunt Joshua let out as his stomach hit the mattress.

"If you don't fuck me in the next two seconds," Joshua warned, and Frank would have loved to know what he intended to do if Frank didn't comply. Except he had no intention of not giving in completely. He carefully but quickly rolled on the condom, then applied a generous amount of lube. With an arm around Joshua's shoulder, Frank used his free hand to line himself up. He pressed the head of his cock against Joshua's hole, then pushed in until he was buried to the hilt. He snapped his hips, and Joshua cried out.

"Yes! Oh God, Frank. Just like that."

"You like that, huh?" Frank snapped his hips again, driving himself in deep before pulling out and plunging in again and again.

"Oh fuck! Yes! Please, Frank."

Frank gave Joshua what he wanted, fucking him fast and hard, the bed moving beneath them as he pounded Joshua's ass, their slick bodies smacking together, the sound mixing with their curses and groans. Having Joshua under him, the sounds he made as Frank gave them both everything they wanted... it was better than Frank could have imagined.

Sweat beaded his brow, his panting breath mingling with Joshua's as he drove himself inside Joshua's tight heat. He took hold of Joshua's chin and turned his face so he could kiss him. It was sloppy and hungry as his hips thrust wildly, all calm and rhythm lost as he chased his climax. His muscles tightened, his body trembling as his orgasm swept through him like a tsunami. He roared as the pleasure exploded into release, the condom filing with his come. A few more thrusts and he hissed as he pulled out of Joshua and fell onto his back, his chest rising and falling with rapid breaths.

Joshua sat back on his heels, his hand working furiously as he jerked himself off.

"Wait. Sit here." Frank tapped his chest, and Joshua let out a delicious little whimper as he quickly scrambled over. He sat on Frank's chest, his moan sinful when Frank opened his mouth. With his knees on either side of Frank's head, his hands on the wall, and his cock down Frank's throat, Joshua fucked Frank's mouth. It didn't take long, not after Frank pressed a finger to Joshua's hole. He cried out and came down Frank's throat. He remained there for a few heartbeats, kneeling over Frank before he dropped onto the bed. He slid down and curled up against Frank, bringing Frank's face toward his to kiss him. He moaned, most likely at the taste of himself on Frank's tongue.

They kissed for ages, Frank on his side facing Joshua and holding him as close against him as he could manage, their legs intertwined. He couldn't remember the last time he'd spent this much time in bed with a guy doing something other than fucking. He'd never felt the need to keep anyone around longer than they had to. Even when he'd been seeing someone, work usually had him getting out of bed and getting on with his day. For the first time since he could remember, he didn't *want* to go anywhere. He wanted to stay right here, like this.

After some thought, Frank blurted out the words lingering on his tongue. "What if we stay in tomorrow?"

Joshua propped himself on his elbow, his boyish smile wide and his blue-green eyes filled with happiness Frank had a hand in giving. "Really?"

"Yeah." Frank mirrored Joshua's position and ran his fingers through Joshua's hair. "We'll stay in bed, spend some time together. I'll try to remember to feed you in between doing terribly dirty things to you."

Joshua laughed and kissed him. "I'd love that."

Love.

The word had Frank's heart in his throat. It was ridiculous, the kind of reaction one little word had on him. Love was something he had no time for, and until this moment, he'd brushed it off as something he didn't need. His life was fine without it. *He* was fine without it. When he wanted sex, he had his pick of men. He had wealth and a business that allowed him to give back, to help those who'd been in the position he'd once been. Did he need to be in love? No. Did he want it with the man in his arms?

"Your eyebrows are looking very stern."

Frank blinked at Joshua. "What?"

With a soft laugh, Joshua gently tapped a finger between Frank's eyebrows. "Your eyebrows. When you're lost in thought, they get very stern-looking. Most people think you're glowering, but you're actually just thinking."

"How do you know?" Frank couldn't help his smile.

Joshua lowered his gaze, a swatch of pink crossing his nose and cheeks. He shrugged. "I've noticed things."

"Oh yeah?" Frank brought Joshua with him as he rolled onto his back. "What things?"

"I'm going to refrain from answering on the grounds that you're going to think I'm a stalker."

Frank hummed. "I see. I guess if that's the case, I should mention how that day at the beach wasn't the first time I noticed you had freckles."

"Oh?"

"Nope. I noticed the day we met, when you let me put my arm around you. They're so faint. You can only see them close up." He brushed a finger over the bridge of Joshua's nose and the light sprinkle of freckles that spread across his nose and cheeks. "I noticed how you do this little happy dance when you think no one is watching, whether you're standing or sitting."

Joshua eyed him. "Were you watching me earlier tonight?"

"I might have momentarily glanced at the camera feed while I was on the phone." Frank couldn't believe what he was about to admit. Was his face as red as it felt? "Seeing you calmed me."

Joshua's expression softened. "Really?"

"Really."

With a hum, Joshua laid his head on Frank's chest, a yawn escaping him. Shit. Frank had forgotten how late it was. Joshua was probably asleep most nights at this time.

"I like that," Joshua replied through another yawn. His head popped up. "Oh my God, here I am in bed with *you* and I'm yawning! I'm so sorry!"

"It's okay," Frank promised him. "It's late, and we've been busy. Let's get some sleep."

Neither of them brought up the fact they were sleeping together in Frank's bed. Not that Frank would have wanted it any other way. Joshua's weight on him, his head lying against Frank's chest as they drifted off to sleep in the middle of his huge king-sized bed, the moonlight from the garden coming in to wash over them... They could have this every night. Maybe... maybe it was time to rethink his life and how Joshua could be a part of it.

SIX

THIS WAS HAPPENING.

It took Joshua a couple of heartbeats to believe what he was seeing. He couldn't help his huge smile as he lay facing the sexy man in front of him. Frank was still asleep, his full lips slightly parted, beard grown in, dark hair beautifully disheveled and falling over his brow. How was it possible for one man to look so damned incredible in the morning?

Careful not to wake Frank, Joshua rolled off the bed, slipped into his boxer-briefs—the only item of his clothing that made it to the bedroom—and found the en suite bathroom. Once he'd peed, he washed his hands and face, pausing to look at himself in the mirror. Oh my God, he was in Frank's house. After having sex with him. Twice. Holy shit! A happy little squeak escaped him, and he clamped his hands over his mouth before shutting his eyes tight and doing a little dance.

"You're adorable."

The yelp Joshua let out was less than flattering. He threw a hand to his heaving chest as Frank barely stifled a laugh. "You scared the shit out of me!"

Frank stood leaning against the bathroom doorway. "Sorry."

"Liar. You're not sorry at all."

"You're right. I'm not." He came up behind Joshua and pulled him back against him. "It was worth seeing you all cute and excited."

Joshua arched an eyebrow at him through the mirror. "Let's not make it a habit. How is it you can sneak up on someone without making a sound?"

"I don't sneak up on people," Frank said with a chuckle. He released Joshua and went to pee. "There's a brand-new toothbrush in the bottom left-hand drawer."

"Thanks. And you so do sneak up on people," Joshua said as he opened the drawer and found the packaged toothbrush. "You scare the shit out of your staff all the time."

Frank finished up, then washed his hands at the

second sink, his smile wicked. "Not my fault they're not paying attention."

"How do you do it?"

Frank shrugged. "Probably from my days working the job."

"The job?"

"The only job." Frank's smile turned wistful. "At least it used to be. Not that I don't love what I do now. It's a lot more pay for a lot less risk, but that wasn't why I became a firefighter. I loved going out there and helping people."

"You still help people," Joshua reminded him before brushing his teeth. Frank did the same at his sink. It was all very... normal and domestic. After drying his hands, Frank wrapped his arms around Joshua from behind again. That's when Joshua noticed the scar on his left shoulder. "Is that why you had to retire from firefighting?" he asked gently, nodding toward the scar.

Frank sighed. "Yeah. It was an accident." He removed a black tube from the little basket to the right of the sink, which Joshua assumed was shaving cream since he also removed his electric shaver from its charger. "We were called out to a townhome that was engulfed. The owner passed out in his bedroom on the second floor after getting drunk, completely forgetting he'd left his fried eggs cooking on the stove downstairs. I was carrying him down the ladder when he came to and lost it. As much as I tried to calm him, he was in hysterics, flailing and fighting me. He punched the side of my helmet. One minute we were struggling, and the next I'm hanging on to the ladder with one arm, holding on to him with the other. The pain was excruciating. It was bad. I dislocated my shoulder and tore my rotator cuff. Two surgeries later and that was it. No more job."

"I'm so sorry, Frank." Joshua turned and leaned against the counter, watching Frank lather up. Whatever it was smelled amazing. God, no wonder he always smelled so damned good.

"Don't be. It led me to where I am today." He kissed Joshua's cheek, making him laugh when he left behind a glop of shaving cream. "I still get to hang out with my best friend, Val, who's now the fire chief. We have barbecues, talk about old times, he tells me about all the stupid shit the rookies do. It's like I never left."

Joshua's heart swelled at Frank's smile. It transformed his whole face. "What is that? It smells incredible."

"It has coconut, chamomile, and sage for your skin, but what you smell is the bergamot and lavender." Frank shrugged. "I like to take care of myself." He turned the electric shaver on and faced the mirror, pausing to look at himself and seeming to get lost in some memory. "When you spend years with nothing, you learn to appreciate life's little luxuries when you can get them."

The tears pooled in Joshua's eyes, and he quickly blinked them away before Frank could see them. He focused on the bathroom instead. "I can't imagine what you went through." Joshua hadn't seen the rest of the house. He'd been too distracted last night by Frank's mouth and hands on him, but if it was anything like the bathroom, he'd bet it was impressive. The huge bathroom was all cream marble with dark wood cabinets and industrial style lighting. The shower had it's own tiled room, the bathtub with jets big enough for two. It was spotless, sleek, sophisticated, and expensive.

"Hey." Frank took hold of Joshua's chin and turned his face so their eyes could meet. Despite the sadness in Joshua's heart, he couldn't help his soft laugh at Frank's half-clean, half-foamed face, which promptly broke into a smile at Joshua's laugh. He tapped a finger to his foamed cheek and plopped a dollop of the cream on the tip of Joshua's nose. "I'm okay. It was a terrifying time for me, and for a long time, I had nightmares I was still that scared teen out on the streets. Now when I look back, it serves as a reminder not to take anything for granted, and to never stop doing what I can to help those youth who are in the same position I was then."

"You're an amazing man," Joshua said, coming to stand behind Frank and wrapping his arms around him. He let his head rest against Frank's back.

"I'm not. I'm just a regular guy who doesn't always get it right but is trying."

"Can I ask you a question?" Joshua could stand here all day watching Frank shave.

"Of course."

"Why a hummingbird?"

Frank's smile turned wistful. "It was a nickname. When I was little, I was a tiny thing, so much smaller than other boys my age, and I had so much energy. I never seemed to stop, always zooming from one place to another. My sister used to laugh and call me a hummingbird. It became her nickname for me."

"What happened to her?" Joshua asked softly, his heart breaking at the sadness that filled Frank's eyes.

Frank finished shaving, washed his face, and patted it dry. He turned in Joshua's arms. "Are you sure you want to hear this?"

Joshua nodded. "But only if you want to share it with me."

"My mother reached out to me only once after I was kicked out, and it was to tell me my sister was dead. During a night out with friends, she was jumped in the parking lot and raped. My mother told me she agreed with the detective that if my sister hadn't been dressed the way she was, maybe it wouldn't have happened. My sister ended up taking her own life." He frowned and stared down at his razor. "I know there's nothing I could have done. My parents had done their best to turn her against me. They cut me out of their lives completely, like I never existed, but I still wish I could have been there for her. To let her know it wasn't her fault. In my mind, she'll always be the loving big sister I looked up to who called me hummingbird."

Joshua placed his hand on Frank's arm, tears stinging the back of his eyes. "I'm so sorry, Frank."

Frank turned and kissed him, a slow, languid kiss, like they had all the time in the world. Or at least it seemed so until Joshua's stomach rumbled.

"Oh my God, I'm so sorry." Mortified, Joshua let his head fall against Frank's chest.

Frank pulled back with a chuckle. "How about

some breakfast? Then I can give you a tour of the house."

"Sounds great." He looked down at himself. "I should probably find my clothes."

"Or you can borrow a pair of yoga pants and a T-shirt." Frank hummed as he leaned in to kiss Joshua again. "I like the idea of you in one of my shirts."

Joshua could barely control his grin. "Okay." He happily accepted the pants and shirt, and although both were a bit baggy and long on him, it wasn't too bad. They were super soft and so comfortable. After they dressed, Joshua followed Frank out into what looked like the formal dining room, and beyond that the kitchen.

"Your house is amazing." It was all high ceilings and big windows that filled the place with sunlight. The kitchen was huge with dark wood cabinets, black marble countertops, and stainless-steel appliances. The sleek industrial style continued with the three large pendant lights that hung from the ceiling over the island counter. "What can I do to help?"

"Grab me the eggs, bacon, and fruit bowl from the fridge. Do you like French toast?"

"I love French toast."

"Perfect. You can help me make it."

Together they worked around the kitchen. Joshua prepared the egg, vanilla, and cinnamon mix for the brioche. He plucked a blueberry out of the fruit bowl, receiving a playful smack on the hand that made him laugh.

"Keep your grabby hands off my berries."

"But I like your berries," Joshua replied, waggling his eyebrows.

"Ooh, you're trouble." Frank dipped two slices of brioche in the mix and placed them in the frying pan. He pointed behind Joshua. "Can you grab me that."

Like a dork, Joshua turned. "What?"

"Never mind," Frank said through a mouthful of something.

"You sneaky sneak! You totally stole some bacon, didn't you?"

Frank shook his head. "I don't know what you're talking about. You left the fridge door open, by the way."

"I did not." Joshua laughed when Frank tried and failed several times to get him to turn around, including taking hold of his shoulder and physically turning him to point out the view from the living room window, which *was* beautiful. "Put the bacon down, Frank."

Crunch.

"Working around Ace has you hearing things," Frank replied with a snicker.

"He's also a bacon thief." Joshua turned around and plucked a blueberry out of the bowl. He tossed it and opened his mouth to catch it, only to have Frank swipe it out of the air and pop it into his mouth. Joshua gasped. "You stole my blueberry!"

"I did," Frank said with a chuckle as he slipped the last piece of French toast onto the plate. "And it was delicious. Probably the best blueberry I have ever tasted. There will never be another blueberry like it."

Joshua barked out a laugh, then shook his head. He helped Frank take their bounty of breakfast goodness to the smaller dining room table at the end of the kitchen. They served themselves coffee, and Frank brought over a carafe of freshly squeezed orange juice. Joshua ate his weight in French toast topped with berries and gooey syrup. He couldn't remember the last time he had this much fun at breakfast. Anyone who knew Frank saw him as this scary, serious guy, but in truth, he was just observant, quiet. How many people outside of Joshua knew Frank had this lighter side to him? Possibly Colton, who'd known Frank for years, and no doubt Frank's best friend, Val.

Once they'd cleaned up breakfast, Frank took him on a tour of the house as promised. It was a two-story five-bedroom house with one of the bedrooms converted into a home office, another into a home gym. The two upstairs bedrooms remained guest rooms, along with a small sitting room and two bathrooms. The place was massive. Not as big as Colton's mansion, but still huge. They stepped through the sliding glass doors in the living room and out onto the patio. Although not on the beach, it had a breathtaking view of the river. All kinds of trees and flowers grew around the property, all expertly taken care of.

"You have a jacuzzi?"

"Yep. Want to take a dip?"

"Oh my God, yes!"

Frank started stripping, and Joshua gaped at him. "What? There's no one around us. Plus, there's a shitload of trees and a fence. We're good."

"Okay." Joshua didn't need to be told twice. He stripped where he stood and followed Frank in. The water was hot, but not so much it was unbearable. He sat and groaned as the jets massaged his back. "This is nice."

"Come here." Frank motioned him over, and Joshua went, smiling when Frank pulled him onto his lap. Their slow kisses soon turned as heated as the water they were in. Frank palmed both their hard erections and jerked them off together until Joshua was screaming Frank's name.

The rest of the day was just as lazy and amazing. At least until a phone call came in during dinner, which they'd made together. Joshua had never had so much fun cooking steaks before. He'd also had no idea Frank loved to cook. They'd put on music, talked, and laughed. It had been wonderful.

"Shit. Okay. I'll be right there."

Looked like dinner was over. Joshua was more worried about the grim expression on Frank's face. He hung up and stood.

"What is it?"

"Fucking pipe burst again. I need to go."

"I'll come with you." Joshua made to stand, but Frank held a hand up to stop him.

"No, it's fine. You finish your dinner. Stay as long as you like."

"Frank—"

"It's fine." Frank wiped his mouth with a napkin, then kissed Joshua. Something flashed in his eyes, something Joshua couldn't quite make out, but it was gone just as soon as it had appeared. Joshua didn't push it. He quickly finished his dinner, even if he didn't have much of an appetite left. Not because Frank was leaving, but because Frank seemed... off.

"I'll see you later." Frank paused by the door, and Joshua hurried over.

"Frank, please. Let me come with you. I'm sure there's something I can do to help."

"Thanks. I had a good time last night." With a kiss to Joshua's cheek, Frank was gone, leaving Joshua feeling weird. Did Frank want him to stay? Was he hoping Joshua would be here when he got home? What was he supposed to do here on his own until Frank got back? He supposed he could watch TV, but who knew what time Frank would be back?

Deciding to stay, Joshua made himself comfortable on the couch. He watched TV for several hours and sent texts to Frank asking him if he was okay. He'd tried calling but Frank never answered or called back. At some point Joshua fell asleep. Checking his phone, he frowned at the time. Five in the morning. Damn. He must have been more tired than he thought. Checking his phone again, his heart sank. Not one call, no texts, nothing. Knowing Colton would be up, Joshua called him.

"Hey."

"Hi."

"What's wrong?"

"Nothing?" Joshua winced. Colton knew him much better than that.

"What happened? Are you okay? Where are you?"

Joshua couldn't help his smile. Colton might be an only child, but that didn't mean he didn't appoint himself big brother. "I'm at Frank's house. We, um, slept together."

"That's great!"

A sigh escaped Joshua.

"That not the sigh of everything's great. Talk to me."

"It was amazing. I mean, it was everything I thought it would be and more. But we were having dinner when a call came in from the club. The pipe in the employee lounge burst again. I offered to come with him, but he told me to finish my dinner and stay as long as I wanted."

"Okay. Where is Frank now?"

"I don't know. I haven't heard from him, Colton. *Ten hours*. I called, texted, and nothing. He couldn't call me or text me in ten hours to tell me he was okay? I know he doesn't have to answer to me, and maybe he only intended for things between us to be just about sex, but for fuck's sake, he couldn't just say *something*?" Joshua shook his head, hating the heaviness in his heart or the way the back of his eyes stung. "I'm worried about him. He's working himself to death and doesn't even realize it. Maybe he doesn't think I'd be worried? God, what if he thinks it was all a mistake?"

"He cares about you," Colton promised.

"I know. At least, I think I know."

"What are you going to do?"

Joshua opened his mouth when he heard the door being unlocked. "I think he's home."

"Okay. You deserve more, Joshua. Remember that."

"Thank you." Joshua hung up. He stood when the lights came on, and Frank stopped, his expression clearly stating he hadn't expected Joshua to be here.

"Joshua?"

"Yeah, I fell asleep. Sorry. You said it was okay if I stayed."

"Of course it's okay. I, uh, just didn't think you'd be here."

"Oh." Joshua nodded his understanding. He probably figured Joshua would have gone home by now. How many guys hung around *that* long after sex? Was he being naïve?

"No, I didn't mean it like that. I'm happy you're here."

"Everything okay at the club?" He hated how awkward things were between them. Frank didn't move from where he stood, and Joshua didn't go to him, unsure if his advances would be welcome. "You didn't call. Or text."

"I know."

Joshua's heart plummeted. "Why?"

"I was kind of busy."

"Right." So basically, Frank had ignored Joshua on purpose. Perfect. After heading to Frank's bedroom, he grabbed his clothes off the bed.

"I didn't mean it like that."

"You did. It's fine." He quickly changed back into his own clothes.

"I knew this would happen."

Joshua paused halfway through buttoning his shirt and lifted his gaze to Frank. "Knew what would happen?"

"What always happens. I start seeing someone, they act like they're okay with my owning a club, and then they start resenting me for it."

What the hell? Where had *that* come from? "Wow, I didn't realize you thought so little of me."

"Come on. You can't tell me it's not true. I know you're upset about today."

"Yes, I'm upset," Joshua spat out as he pulled on his shoes. "Not because you had to go deal with an emergency at the club, but because you shut me out, let me worry about you for *ten* hours because you couldn't spare the half a minute it took to answer my call or text just to let me know you were okay. To make matters worse, you're accusing me of having feelings that I don't even have and dismissing me without giving me a chance."

This couldn't be happening. No, it was fine. It *had* to be fine. He just needed some time away from Frank, and maybe Frank simply needed some time on his own. So much had happened in the last few days alone, Joshua needed to cut the guy a break. Joshua went into the living room and grabbed his jacket up off the couch. "If I'm feeling a certain way, believe me, you'll know it." He headed for the door, his heart sinking when Frank didn't so much as utter a word. Turning, he shook his head. "If all you want is sex, just say so. I'm a big boy; I can handle it." He slammed the door behind him and shoved his arms into his jacket.

The door opened behind him, and Frank

growled, "Where the fuck are you going? I drove you here, remember?"

Joshua narrowed his eyes at Frank. "I can get myself home. Thanks for the concern." He ignored Frank and hurried down the stairs. Taking out his phone, he called Colton. "Can you send a car to pick me up? I'm coming in to work today."

"Of course I can send someone. I'm so sorry."

"Me too." He hung up and sighed. This wasn't how he pictured things going between them, but that was the nature of relationships, wasn't it? Not that they had a relationship. Sort of. *Ugh*, okay, no. All he needed was some time to regroup. He wasn't giving up on Frank. Not yet. This was only a hiccup. Maybe he needed to add a new tab to his spreadsheet. *How not to strangle your man in five easy steps.* Something told him it would take more than five steps.

SEVEN

"YOU'RE AN ASSHOLE, YOU KNOW THAT?"

"Excuse me?" Frank lifted his gaze from his computer to the very annoying man sitting on his couch glaring at him. He should have kicked Ace out when he walked in here like he owned the place. Did he think he could do whatever the hell he wanted because he was married to Colton? Who the hell was Frank kidding? His friends were a pain in the ass, and they were very aware he wouldn't do a damn thing about it.

"You are an asshole," Ace repeated, enunciating each word.

"I know that. Are you expecting me to get offended, or... what? What do you want, Sharpe?" As if he didn't already know. "Colton sent you."

"Colton is perfectly capable of telling you what a fuckwit you are on his own. I'm sure he'll be along shortly. I'm here because my husband is unhappy, and my husband is unhappy because his friend is unhappy."

Frank ignored the way his heart squeezed in his chest at hearing Ace's words. He'd never meant to hurt Joshua, but they were heading in that direction anyway, so why prolong it? "I didn't think Joshua was the kind of guy to have someone fight his battles for him."

"Again, you're an ass. He doesn't know, and he'll probably be pissed when he finds out, but Jesus, Frank, what the hell is wrong with you?"

"You seem to have a pretty good idea. Why don't you tell me?"

"Joshua is crazy about you. You *knew* that. Why would you fuck him and just toss him aside?"

"Fuck you," Frank spat, jumping from his chair. "I did not fuck him and toss him aside."

"No?" Ace leaned back and threw his arms open. "You could have fooled me."

"It's none of your fucking business."

"But it is *my* business," Colton hissed as he marched into the room and stopped in front of

Frank. "Joshua is a kind, sweet, wonderful person. He doesn't deserve you shitting all over his heart."

"Joshua is a grown man who doesn't need you two mother hens trying to fix his ouchies. Mind your own fucking business."

Colton narrowed his eyes, and Frank cursed under his breath. Great. Nothing and no one was more of a pain in the ass, or diva, than a pissed-off Colton.

"Now you listen to me. You're going to fix this."

Frank opened his mouth to reply, but Colton held up a finger to stop him. "I love you, you know I do, but right now, you're being an ass. One thing you have never been is a coward. Don't start now. You care about him. I know you do."

Feeling deflated, Frank dropped down onto his chair. "That's not enough to make a relationship work."

"Bullshit. For the first time in your life, you've found someone who can hurt you, really hurt you, and you're scared. No one understands that better than I do, believe me." Colton's blue-gray eyes filled with love as he turned to his husband, his smile radiant. "I took a chance, Frank, and I have never been more grateful that I did."

Ace stood and joined his husband to pull him

into his arms. He grabbed Colton, dipped him, making him laugh, and kissed him.

"You're both disgusting," Frank grumbled.

"You too can be disgusting," Ace said with a big dopey smile as he pulled Colton back up with him. "With Joshua."

"You're not going to let this drop, are you?"

Ace put a hand to his heart. "What kind of friends would we be if we didn't meddle in your life? If it weren't for me, King would have never admitted he was in love with Leo. I united those two love doves." He brought his hands up, fluttering his fingers, then laced them together. "I'm a love master."

Frank was unimpressed. "Love master, huh? Weren't you the one who fell in love with your client while on the job?"

"Client's son," Ace corrected. He blew Colton a kiss. "It worked out for the best."

"Right. After your brothers-in-arms, who you kept your secret love affair from, had to help you clean up your mess when your client found out."

Ace pursed his lips. "You know, it's that kind of negativity that's going to keep you from your love dove." He fluttered his fingers once more, but before he could lace them together, Frank jutted a finger toward the door.

"Get out of my office."

"Okay." Ace kissed Colton's cheek. "I leave the grumpy dove in your hands." He hurried out of Frank's office.

"At what point did you think marrying a man who refers to people as love doves seemed like a good idea?"

Colton laughed. "He's nuts. I know that." He shoved his hands into his pockets and shrugged. "I wouldn't change a thing. The way that man loves me?" He shook his head. "No one's ever made me feel as cherished."

Frank nodded his agreement. As over-the-top as Ace was, the guy had a heart of gold. Hell, he'd almost died for Colton, and they all knew Ace wouldn't hesitate to do it again. There was nothing on this earth Anston Sharpe wouldn't do for the man he loved. Frank could have that, if he wanted it.

"Just... think about it, Frank. It's not too late." Colton patted Frank's shoulder, then left.

What the hell was wrong with him? Colton and Ace were right. Joshua had the power to really hurt him, so the first opportunity Frank had to leave, he took it. Fuck, he was such a coward. Was he really going to let Joshua walk out of his life because he was too scared to take a risk? The fact he was this scared should have told him how much Joshua meant to him. His laugh held no humor.

"Un-fucking-believable." He'd spent years running into burning buildings. His entire fucking life had been one risk after another, and now when he needed to get his shit together and go for it, he'd let his fear get the better of him. He needed to call Joshua and fix this. A knock on his door stopped him reaching for his cellphone. "Now what? Yeah?"

Seth opened the office door and stuck his head in. "Jack and Joker are here."

Ah, the dastardly duo. "What mischief have they come to unleash in my club?"

"I don't know, but they have their bestest boy with them."

Frank couldn't help his smile. "Bring him in through the back." Just because he couldn't have Chip in the club, didn't mean he couldn't sneak the beautiful boy in through the back of house. Seth nodded excitedly and was off, making Frank chuckle. His staff had met Chip during the Four Kings Security annual charity gala a few months back. He'd been an added bonus during the bachelor auction when Joker had gone up on stage to be auctioned. As if one cute guy hadn't been enough, the crowd had lost their fucking minds when the spirited black Belgian Malinois took the stage. Joker ended up raising the most money in the history of the event.

A bark had him turning in his chair, a huge smile on his face when the door opened and Chip came bounding over like a giant black bunny. With the size of his ears, he certainly could get mistaken for a rabbit. They were glorious.

"Hello, fella. Who's a handsome boy?"

Chip barked and sat in front of Frank to get ear scratches.

"That's right. *You're* handsome."

"Frank, thank God you're okay," Jack said, hurrying over to Frank's side.

"What? Yeah, of course. What's going on?"

Joker stepped up next to his best friend and partner in crime. The non-furry one. "Have you heard from Troy Ross?"

At the mention of the name, Frank glowered, though not as darkly as Jack, who balled his fists at his sides. "That son of a bitch? No. Not since I kicked him out for trying to take advantage of Fitz. Why?" What a mess it had been. The night of the bachelor auction, someone had targeted Jack's boyfriend, Fitz, drugging him in the hopes of getting Jack away from him. And Troy Ross, one of Frank's clients, had found Fitz, and instead of being a decent human being, decided to be an asshole. Jack had punched the guy in the face, and Frank had revoked his club membership and kicked him out on his ass.

"He's the one behind the raid," Jack said.

"What?" Frank stood, his blood boiling.

Jack nodded. "The judge? He's an old golfing buddy of Ross's father. It took some digging, but we were able to make the connection. The thing is, no one's heard from Ross in weeks. That night at the club started a chain reaction."

"There were business associates here with him that night," Joker continued. "They were embarrassed and appalled by his behavior. They ended up cancelling contracts. Word spread and the guy started fucking up all over the place. Got in deep with the wrong people. He lost his business, and my gut says he's gunning for you, Frank."

"I can handle Ross."

Jack shook his head. "A rich guy who's lost everything and blames you? He's desperate. Who knows what this guy is capable of? You should probably tell Joshua. He was in the VIP section with Colton a few minutes ago."

Frank's heart slammed in his chest. "Joshua's here?"

"Yeah, he came with Colton," Joker replied. "I was with Jack when the intel came through. We stopped to talk to you before we head back to HQ to speak to Mason. Until the police locate Ross, we need to reassess the club's security."

"Fine. Do whatever you need to do." He gave Chip one last scratch before heading for his office door. "I need to talk to Joshua." They walked out into the hall, the double doors that led into the club swinging open. Frank had been about to thank the guys when Chip sniffed the air, then bolted toward the swinging doors and into the club. "Shit. Your dog just took off."

Joker's eye went wide. "Fuck. We need to evacuate."

"What?"

"Get everyone out of the club," Joker yelled as he took off after Chip.

That's when Frank remembered what Chip had been trained for, what his job at Four Kings Security was.

Detecting explosives.

Frank snatched his radio off his belt as he bolted toward the double doors, Jack on his heels.

"Security, get everyone out *now*. Protocol signal thirty." By the time he was on the floor, security was quickly and calmly moving everyone to the exits. Where the hell was Colton? Joshua would be difficult to spot, but at six foot five, Colton was easier to find. Spotting Colton, Frank headed toward the VIP area.

"Calling it in now," Jack said, phone to his ear. "Where the hell are you going?"

"I need to find Joshua. He's somewhere in the club."

Jack grabbed his arm. "Frank, if this guy's targeting you—"

"I'm not leaving without Joshua," Frank growled. Thankfully, Jack released him. They headed for Colton, and Frank's heart dropped when he saw Ace but not Joshua.

"Where's Joshua?" Frank asked.

"He went to the men's room," Colton said. "Ace got a call from Joker. He said Chip found something in one of the back rooms. He's clearing everyone out."

"Okay." Frank turned to Ace. "Get him outside to safety. I'm going to find Joshua."

Ace shook his head. "He's probably already outside, Frank. You need to leave the building."

Frank met Ace's eyes. "Would you leave Colton's safety to chance?"

With pursed lips, Ace shook his head.

"I didn't think so." Frank turned and pushed through the crowd, calling out over his shoulder. "Take Colton outside."

Knowing Ace would keep Colton safe, Frank hurried against the current of men toward the men's room. He threw the door open and froze.

"Ross?"

"Hi, Frank." Troy Ross waved at him, a gun in his hand, but there was no sign of Joshua. Frank prayed he'd made it outside. "Nice of you to remember me."

"How the hell did you get in here?"

"One of the construction workers let me in. He believed me when I told him I'd left my wallet inside but couldn't go in through the front in case my date saw me. I was skipping out on account of it being a disaster. Which pretty much defines my life, thanks to you. Do you have any idea what you did to me?"

"You signed a contract. You knew the rules, knew what would happen if you broke them."

"Come on, Frank. You saw the way he was dressed. If not me, it would have been someone else. What do you care?"

Ross's words sent a fierce rage through Frank. "I *care* because you're a vile predator. I *care* because someone just like you raped my sister. I *care* because I wasn't there to stop her from killing herself after she was told she'd asked for it. I *care* because as long as guys like you exist, I will take joy in putting you behind bars, or in the case of my sister's rapist, in the hospital, *then* behind bars."

"Poor Frank." Ross pretended to cry. "Always too late to save the one he loves."

A chill went up Frank's spine. "What are you talking about?"

"Couldn't save your sister. Can't save your boyfriend."

Frank took a step forward. "So help me, if you've hurt him—"

"You'll do nothing, Frank. Like you did nothing to help your sweet sister."

"Fuck you!" He lunged at Ross, only to have the gun thrust in his face.

"Let's take a little walk."

"No."

"If you want to see Joshua, you'll take a walk with me, Frank." He motioned toward the door with the gun.

Frank turned and left the men's room, Ross close behind.

"The room all the way at the end on the right."

Doing as Ross said, Frank headed down the hall, the doors on either side belonging to the back rooms open and empty. A familiar scent caught his nose, and his heart all but stopped when he spotted the faint wisps of smoke coming from under the last door on the right.

"No." Frank bolted to the door, skidding to a stop in front of it, the curtain of the small glass window open. Terror filled him as he stared at Joshua pressing himself into the far-left corner of the room, the right side engulfed in flames. "Joshua!"

At hearing his name, Joshua's head shot up, the fear in his eyes something Frank would never forget. Relief quickly followed, and Joshua ran to the door.

"Frank! The door won't open!"

"I'm going to get you out of there," Frank promised.

"You shouldn't lie to him, Frank."

Fury filled him as he spun toward Ross. "What the hell did you do? Open this door, right now!"

Ross's laugh sounded unhinged.

Frank remembered his training. As much as it killed him, he had to approach this the way he would have when he was still part of Fire Rescue. He slowly held his hands up in front of him.

"Troy, I'm sorry for what happened to you. I never wanted this. Please, let me help you."

"How are you going to do that, Frank? Are you going to recover my business? All my clients? What about my house? You going to kick out the asshole that lives there now? How exactly are you going to help me?"

"We can discuss this, get you help. You've been through a lot." To Frank's left he could hear Joshua coughing. He didn't have long before the fire spread, and he had even less time before the smoke would damage Joshua's lungs, then kill him. "Troy, you can still turn this around. Joshua didn't hurt anyone. Whatever revenge you want, I'm right here, but leave Joshua out of this."

Ross appeared to think about it, then shrugged. "Nah, I think I'm going to watch you watch your boyfriend die and your precious club go up in flames. A very apropos ending, don't you think?"

The police and fire department had been called and were most likely on their way, but Joshua didn't have that much time.

"Frank!"

Frank put his hand to the door beside the

window where he could meet Joshua's gaze. "I'm so sorry, sweetheart. I'm sorry I hurt you. It's going to be okay. You're going to be okay."

Joshua's eyes widened, and he shook his head. "Frank, don't. Please."

Frank turned to face Ross. He ignored Joshua's hoarse pleading and the way he slammed his hands on the door to get Frank's attention.

"I won't let you hurt him."

"Nothing you can do."

Frank started removing his suit jacket.

"What the hell are you doing?"

Everything happened in a heartbeat. Frank tossed his jacket in Ross's face and lunged, grabbing the gun with his left hand and punching the guy across the face with his right. The gun went off, a searing pain in his side making Frank cry out, but he didn't let go of the gun. They struggled, and Frank could feel the blood soaking through his shirt. He punched Ross again, and the gun went off a second time. This time, Ross crumbled to the ground, blood pooling beneath his head.

Snatching the gun up off the floor, he placed his left hand to his side and hurried to the door. "Stand back!"

Joshua ran to the corner of the room, and Frank

shot at the lock. It didn't help that the bastard must have somehow sealed parts of the door. Tossing the gun on the floor, Frank inhaled deeply, fortified himself, and slammed his good side into the door.

"Frank!"

The door creaked but didn't open. He did it again, crying out when his wound tore a little more.

"Frank, stop!"

No way. Instead, Frank slammed into the door over and over until the thing splintered and swung open. Joshua ran to his side in time to stop Frank from hitting the floor.

"Oh my God, he shot you!"

"We need to get out of here," Frank murmured. In the distance he heard shouting and barking. He smiled as Joshua slipped an arm around his waist. They hurried out of the back rooms just as the fire crew arrived. Joshua told them about Ross on the floor in the back. Outside, Frank welcomed the brisk winter air. He closed his eyes, brushed his lips over Joshua's brow, and murmured quietly, "You're my love dove."

"What?" Joshua asked, bemused. "Frank? Frank!"

It was all Frank heard before the darkness came for him.

EIGHT

THREE WEEKS LATER.

"It looks amazing." Joshua stood by the VIP section and stared at the gorgeous display of winter out in the club—from the huge sparkling snowflakes and clear baubles filled with glitter in Sapphire Sands' signature blue that hung from the ceiling, to the faux ice sculptures of frolicking reindeer and white trees with twinkling white lights. The whole thing was magical, like something out of a winter fairy tale.

"Thanks to you," Frank said, wrapping his arms around Joshua from behind. Joshua turned in his arms and smiled up at him. To think how close he'd come to losing Frank.

Being trapped in that room engulfed in flames, with no way to get out, had been the first most terrifying moment of his life. Seeing Frank bleeding out after Troy shot him had been the second. Thankfully, it had been a clean shot, the bullet having gone straight through, away from any vital organ. Frank had been lucky. He'd also been questioned over Troy's death by the same asshole detective who'd raided the club. The detective had tried to make it sound like Frank's prejudice against men like Troy had led to the shooting. Frank's lawyer and Ward Kingston had stepped in and eviscerated the guy, who'd made the mistake of letting slip more than one derogatory remark against Frank's sexuality and ethnicity. He'd be lucky to still have job by the time Frank was done with him.

Once Joshua was sure Frank was okay, he'd lost his shit. Frank had listened to Joshua rant and rave about how he could have died, then promptly told Joshua it had been worth it. Then he laid a truth bomb on Joshua that made his knees weak, and his heart immediately surrendered.

They'd talked, Frank promised to take his

recovery seriously, Joshua kissed him, and Frank had passed out from the meds they were giving him.

"I thought you were going to take a nap," Joshua said, eyebrow arched.

Frank wrinkled his nose. "I got bored."

"The agreement was, you could be here tonight if you took it easy." He gave his boyfriend a pointed look, which clearly wasn't intimidating in the least since Frank merely chuckled.

"I will nap. I promise. First, I want a dance with you."

Joshua eyed him. "Did you forget you're still in recovery from having been shot?"

"Believe me, I haven't forgotten." Frank brushed his lips over Joshua's. "I also haven't forgotten my promise to you."

Joshua couldn't help but smile against Frank's lips. "I might need a little reminder. First tell me what you said before your promise."

With a soft laugh, Frank cupped Joshua's face, brushing his thumb over Joshua's cheek. "You mean how I was a fool for letting you walk away? How I was scared because for the first time I was falling in love with someone who held so much power over me? That?"

Joshua met Frank's gaze and sighed dreamily. "Yeah, that."

"I'm falling hard for you, Joshua. Have been from the day we met. You're amazing, beautiful, and I like who I am when I'm with you."

Joshua's smile couldn't get any bigger. "I feel the same about you, Frank. That day we met, when you opened your arms to me, my heart was yours." He slipped his arms around Frank's neck and kissed him, laughing against his lips at the cheers and catcalls from their friends at the table behind them.

"About damn time," Ace called out. "I knew he was your love dove."

Joshua frowned up at Frank. "Wait, that's what you said before you passed out that night."

"Don't ask," Frank said through a groan. "Don't encourage him."

"Love doves are your person. Your soul mate."

Joshua eyed Ace dubiously as the guy did something weird with his hands. Were those supposed to be wings? Why were they interlacing? What was happening right now?

Leo snickered from beside King. "You know doves are basically just smaller pigeons."

"Only Ace would equate a flying rat with love," Joker said, shaking his head.

"Doves are not flying rats," Ace argued. "But then I shouldn't be surprised. You wouldn't know love if it—"

"Shit on his head," Jack teased. Fitz smacked his boyfriend playfully on the arm. "Leave poor Ace alone. He's a romantic."

"Is that what we're callin' it?" Mason asked, his arm around Lucky, who tried and failed to hide his laughter.

They were a goofy bunch, but Joshua loved them. He lifted his gaze to Frank's and cooed. "And you're my love dove."

Frank's groan made everyone laugh. He was so never going to live that down.

"Why don't you join us?" Red asked, his arm around his boyfriend, Laz.

"Maybe later," Joshua said. "Someone promised they'd take it easy and have been doing everything but, since the club opened."

Joker's eyes suddenly went huge, and he shoved at Jack. "Move."

"What? Stop pushing me. What's the matter with you?"

"I need to get out," Joker said through his teeth. "Move your fucking ass, Constantino."

Joshua searched the floor around them. There

was only one thing—or rather *person*—who would have Joker ready to cause bodily harm if they didn't let him escape. Spotting the tall, elegant dark-haired man heading their way, Joshua held back a smile. Frank cocked his head in question, and Joshua motioned behind him. Frank turned, his frown turning into a wicked smile.

Giovanni Galanos.

Laz's big brother, Gio, was a handsome philanthropist and billionaire. He was also the man who'd won Joker in the bachelor auction. No one knew what happened on their date, and no one dared ask Joker. He might be the smallest of the group, but like the Kings and Jack, he was a former Green Beret. Joker was as volatile as the explosives he and his best boy, Chip, were trained to deal with.

"So help me, Jack, if you don't move, I will climb over your ass."

As Gio approached the table, Joker scrambled over Jack and Fitz, ignoring their protests. He fell forward, only to be caught by Gio.

"Hello, Sacha," Gio said with a smile, his voice smooth and sexy. "So good to have you in my arms again."

Everyone's mouth dropped open.

Again?

"I thought you wanted me to take a nap," Frank whispered in Joshua's ear.

Joshua waved a hand at him. "In a minute. This is better than reality TV." Someone *had* to know what happened on the date. Why had Joker changed his mind? The whole thing had been called off, and then suddenly it was back on, but Joker wouldn't say a word about it, and he was still avoiding Gio like the plague. What the hell was going on between these two?

Gio placed Joker on his feet, his smile never leaving his face as Joker glowered at him.

"I told you not to call me that," Joker spat out.

"Yes, you've been telling me that since we first spoke."

"And yet?" Joker threw his arms up. "Why are you here?"

"Because you're here."

Joker stared at him. "Bullshit."

"Such language," Gio tsked.

"Like I give a fuck. Why are you here?"

It was like the most fascinating tennis match in existence. Their eyes were glued to the two, and Joshua for one couldn't wait to see what gave, because *something* had to give with them.

Gio opened his mouth to answer, but Joker put a hand up to stop him.

"You know what? I don't care. I'm leaving."

"Running away again?"

Joker stopped in his tracks. He turned, and Joshua took a small step behind Frank. If looks could kill, Gio would have been reduced to nothing but ash.

"Don't flatter yourself. I'm going to get a drink." With that he turned and headed for the bar.

"Excuse us," Frank said. "Gio, everyone, it's good to see you. We'll be back in a bit."

Before Joshua could say anything, Frank ushered him toward the back of house.

"But it was just getting good," Joshua said with a huff.

"Security feed in my office, remember? We can watch from a safe distance."

"Ooh, good idea. Should we make some popcorn?"

Frank threw his head back and laughed. He opened one of the double doors for Joshua, then followed him into his office, where he closed the door behind him.

"Gio is a brave man," Frank said, walking to his desktop. He tapped a few keys and the screen showed their friends' table. Gio had taken a seat at the end next to Fitz, leaving only one spot open for Joker. The one next to him.

"I blame the Kings," Frank muttered.

"Why?"

"There's something about them that seems to spread the madness."

It was Joshua's turn to laugh. He couldn't refute it, though. Life had certainly become more colorful since meeting the Kings. But right now, he was focused on the one man who'd made the biggest difference in his life. He took Frank's hand and led him over to the couch. They sat down, and Joshua's heart skipped a beat when Frank pulled him close against him.

"Thank you," Frank said, kissing Joshua.

"For what?"

"For taking a chance on me, risking your heart."

"I could say the same. You're such an amazing man, Frank."

Frank took Joshua's hand in his. "I promise to always listen and to share my worries with you, to never shut you out."

The joy in Joshua's heart overflowed, and he wrapped his arms around Frank, bringing him in for a kiss. He'd wanted this for so long, dreamed of

Frank's kisses, of his arms around Joshua. Now that Joshua had him, he intended to never let go.

It had been a gamble for both of them, but in the end, they'd followed their hearts and found their love dove.

***

LOOKING for the next explosive romance in **The Kings: Wild Cards** series? Check out Joker and Gio's love story, ***Sleight of Hand***, The Kings: Wild Cards book three, now available on Amazon and KindleUnlimited.

***

READ WHERE IT ALL STARTED. ***Love in Spades*** is the first book in the **Four Kings Security** series and Ace and Colton's love story. It's also where Frank and Joshua first met. Available on Amazon and KindleUnlimited.

A NOTE FROM THE AUTHOR

Thank you so much for reading *Raising the Ante*, the second book in The Kings: Wild Cards series. I hope you enjoyed Frank and Joshua's story, and if you did, please consider leaving a review on Amazon. Reviews can have a significant impact on a book's visibility on Amazon, so any support you show these fellas would be amazing. Ready for Joker and Gio's book? Check out, *Sleight of Hand*, book 3 in The Kings: Wild Cards series, available on Amazon and KindleUnlimited.

Haven't read the Kings? Start with *Love in Spades*, available on Amazon and Kindle Unlimited.

Want to stay up-to-date on my releases and receive exclusive content? Sign up for my newsletter.

Follow me on Amazon to be notified of a new

releases, and connect with me on social media, including my fun Facebook group, Donuts, Dog Tags, and Day Dreams, where we chat books, post pictures, have giveaways, and more!

Looking for inspirational photos of my books? Visit my book boards on Pinterest.

Thank you again for joining The Kings: Wild Cards on their adventures. We hope to see you soon!

ALSO BY CHARLIE COCHET

FOUR KINGS SECURITY UNIVERSE

STANDALONE TITLES

Beware of Geeks Bearing Gifts

FOUR KINGS SECURITY SERIES

Love in Spades

Be Still My Heart

Join the Club

Diamond in the Rough

LOCKE AND KEYES AGENCY SERIES

Kept in the Dark

THE KINGS: WILD CARDS SERIES

Stacking the Deck

Raising the Ante

Sleight of Hand

RUNAWAY GROOMS SERIES

Aisle Be There

THIRDS UNIVERSE

THIRDS SERIES

Hell & High Water

Blood & Thunder

Rack & Ruin

Rise & Fall

Against the Grain

Catch a Tiger by the Tail

Smoke & Mirror

Thick & Thin

Darkest Hour Before Dawn

Gummy Bears & Grenades

Tried & True

THIRDS BEYOND THE BOOKS SERIES

THIRDS Beyond the Books Volume 1

THIRDS Beyond the Books Volume 2

THIRDS: REBELS SERIES

Love and Payne

Disarming Donner

Courage and the King

North Pole City Tales Complete Series Boxset

STANDALONE TITLES

Forgive and Forget

Love in Retrograde

AUDIOBOOKS

Check out the audio versions on Audible.

ABOUT THE AUTHOR

Charlie Cochet is the international bestselling author of the THIRDS series. Born in Cuba and raised in the US, Charlie enjoys the best of both worlds, from her daily Cuban latte to her passion for classic rock.

Currently residing in Central Florida, Charlie is at the beck and call of a rascally Doxiepoo bent on world domination. When she isn't writing, she can usually be found devouring a book, releasing her creativity through art, or binge watching a new TV series. She runs on coffee, thrives on music, and loves to hear from readers.

www.charliecochet.com

Sign up for Charlie's newsletter:
https://newsletter.charliecochet.com

facebook.com/charliecochet

twitter.com/charliecochet

instagram.com/charliecochet

bookbub.com/authors/charliecochet

goodreads.com/CharlieCochet

pinterest.com/charliecochet

Made in the USA
Middletown, DE
16 July 2022

69514353R00080